I0763440

Arcturus

MICHAEL COMBS

Edited by Gwendolynn Combs of Penned & Polished

Book layout by Evernight Designs

Front cover photo by Gwendolynn Combs

Back cover photos by Tobias Weinhold and Ross van der Wal via Unsplash.

Cover design by Michael Combs

ISBN: 978-1-7359703-0-1

ACKNOWLEDGMENTS

First, I want to thank my wife Gwen. She somehow stayed patient with me through the editing process. She also introduced me to St. George Island and all our travels from the book.

My children Rachel M. Combs, Kayla N. Combs, and Phoenix N. Millen contributed inspiration.

My mother Glenda Combs always encouraged me to write.

Finally, my father Mitchell Combs: He truly was the best father anyone could have. I wrote Arcturus shortly after his passing. This book is about healing, and at the time I had no idea the impact it would have on me. I hope all who read it experience the same.

This book is dedicated to all the brave souls and their families, the ones who have fought, and those still fighting.

IN OUR LIVES, there are defining moments - moments in which we love, laugh, grieve, and heal. These moments are filled with highs and lows like the ocean tide. When the tide recedes, exposing beautiful shells, only then do we realize the gifts that they bring to us. If it were not for the lows, those gifts would never be discovered.

We all have our own stories, but something truly special happened thirty-six years ago. We received a gift. Her name was Emily Rene White, and this is her story.

AWAY WE GO

Thump, thump, thump, we hear in the darkness before dawn as the luggage wheels drop to each step of the staircase, like a boulder tumbling slowly down a mountain. Halfway down, nine-year-old Nichole stops with one hand on the handle of the suitcase and the other clutching a jar close to her chest, listening to make sure no one is awake. Hearing no movement, she continues her descent.

As the sun rises, we hear Daniel White calling out. "Nichole! Has anyone seen Nichole?" He passes by the kitchen island in their two-story West Hollywood home. Daniel, is a little over six feet tall and has a broad chest and dark hair, with a slight amount of gray sprinkled in. He climbs the stairs to his youngest daughter Nichole's bedroom, finding no trace of her or her luggage. Leaving Nichole's room, he walks down the hall to his thirteen-year-old daughter Michelle's bedroom. Walking around the corner into her room, Daniel seems surprised as Michelle is sitting on the edge of her bed next to her open suitcase, only half packed. As usual, she has her face buried into her iPad.

"Hey! Are you not packed yet?" Daniel asks, and Michelle rolls her eyes, looking up at the ceiling and then to her suitcase in frustration. "Come on. We need to get the bus loaded. We have a lot of road ahead of us. I would like to get to the Grand Canyon while we still have some light left to set up camp. What did I come up here for anyway? Oh yeah... Have you seen your sister?"

"Not since I kicked her out of my room last night. Can I bring my bed and the air conditioner?"

"Ahhh... No."

"Pleaseee? I sooo hate camping. Why can't we stay in a hotel like normal people? I don't want to sleep on the ground."

"Because, first, we are not normal. Normal is overrated. Second, we need to get more in touch with nature. It will do us some good. I promise. Come on! Get going."

"All right..."

"Get moving! Chop chop. Come on! We need to get on the road." He walks down to his five-year-old son Niles's bedroom. He finds Niles sitting on the floor, wearing his Beats headphones and playing with his Captain America figure.

"Hey, buddy, have you seen Nichole?" Niles shakes his head no. "Okay. Well, get your stuff ready so I can take it downstairs to load the bus." Daniel steps downstairs, again calling out, "Nichole!"

On his way outside to look for her, his cell phone rings. Looking at his caller ID, he sees it is his boss Mark Thomas. Daniel, born and raised in Silicon Valley, followed in his father's footsteps in the computer field. Daniel is a corporate IT security trainer with Mitchell-Davis Cyber Security Consultants. He answers his phone. "Hey, Mark. How are you doing? By the way, thank you again for the new sleeping bags and the family tent."

"No problem, Daniel. I just wanted give you a call to wish you and your family the best on your trip."

"Thank you again, Mark, for giving me the time to go."

"Daniel, you have earned this sabbatical. You have sacrificed so much for our company. There is no way I can express my appreciation for everything you have done. Just enjoy this time with your family, and enjoy the beach. I do not want to see you back here in the office until next month, understood?"

"Thank you so much, Mark." Daniel is suddenly startled, for behind him is Niles, blowing the referee whistle that he always wears around his neck.

"Daniel, it sounds like you have your hands full there. I will let you go. Have a great trip, my friend."

Daniel is trying to speak over Niles's whistle. "Thanks, Mark. Yeah, how could you tell? I will see you in August, Mark. Take care."

"You too, Daniel. Be safe."

"Daniel ends the call and looks down at Niles. "What's up, Little Buddy?" Niles is pointing outside to the garage. "Did you find your sister?" Niles shakes his head yes. "Thanks, Little Man." Daniel says, as he pats Niles on the head. "Go get your stuff ready. Remember, only bring two toys."

Daniel walks out to the garage, where the red 1973 Volkswagen Bus he has had since high school is parked. Daniel is tremendously proud of his bus, and over the years he has put several thousand dollars into restoring it. Somewhere along the way, he had lost count of the exact dollar figure; however, his wife Emily often reminded him. Fully restored, he was recently offered forty thousand dollars in cash for it. He turned it down, saying you cannot place a price on its sentimental value. He opens the garage door, discovering the side of the bus has been left open. He sees Nichole in the back seat with her suitcase and the teal clay jar that never leaves her side. He nonchalantly kicks the big white-wall tires. Looking at her, he says softly, "So, what's up, Buttercup? You know it is still a little early to be in there, right?"

Nichole replies, "I know, but I don't want to be left at home like that little Home Alone kid."

Daniel just laughs at her as he reaches in to pick her up, placing her on the ground. "Do not worry, little one. I promise, I will not leave you."

Sticking out her little finger she says, "You pinky promise?"

Daniel wraps his little finger around hers. "I pinky promise. Now, go in the kitchen, and clean up your cereal." At that moment, an SUV pulls up and honks its horn. "Hey, look. Aunt Bev is here with Nathan."

Beverly is Daniel's older sister. Her husband Michael was a Sergeant First Class with the 1st Special Forces Operational Detachment Delta of the United States Army. He was killed four years ago in Afghanistan. She moved back to California from North Carolina following her husband's untimely death. With her is her son Nathan. Nathan was a great kid who never got into any trouble until the death of his father. Having just turned eighteen, Nathan leaves behind a lengthy juvenile record that included drug possession, theft of property, and vandalism, among other lesser charges. He has been told he has a chance now for a fresh start. Daniel and Beverly both agreed it would do Nathan well to go with Daniel's family on their trip to the east coast to get him away from the temptations surrounding him here in Los Angeles.

Beverly steps out of her Cadillac Escalade, calling out to Daniel and Nichole. "Hey, strangers."

Nichole, carrying her jar with her, runs over to Beverly to hug her. "Aunt Bev, I love you so much."

Hugging her back, Beverly says, "I love you, too, Squirt. You are growing way too fast." Then, looking over at Daniel, she asks "And how are you, Little Brother?" as she hugs him.

"I'm just trying to get all these kids ready to go." Looking down at Nichole, Daniel says, "This one is definitely ready. Now, I just have to round up the rest of them." Motioning his head over to her SUV, where Nathan is still sitting and brushing his long hair out of his eyes, Daniel asks, "How's he doing?"

"So far, okay. He has only been eighteen a week, and so far, so good." She motions to her SUV and calls out, "Come on."

Nathan gets out with his duffle bag and walks past Daniel to get into the bus. Daniel says, "Hello, Nathan," with no response other than a nod. Looking back at Beverly and laughing, Daniel says, "What is it about teenagers and their manners these days?"

Beverly says, "Just you wait. It gets worse. And you have three of them to go through."

"Yeah, I know. Don't remind me. Anything I need to know? Medicines? Anything?"

"He is good at taking his antidepressants. Other than that, just take care of all of them and yourself."

"I will do my best. I always do."

"This is going to be a highly emotional trip for all of you, but I know you can do this, Daniel."

"Thanks, Bev."

"You sure you don't want to fly? It would be much faster."

"No. I know. Emily specifically told me to drive the bus. With her, there is no telling what she has cooked up for us."

"My heart is with you, Daniel." Beverly says as she hugs him.

"Want me to go get Michelle and Niles so you can see them before you leave?"

Looking at her watch, she says, "No, I need to get to work. Tell them I love them." She goes to step into the bus to hug Nathan, and he shakes his head no. "No? Okay. You be good. Don't give Uncle Daniel any trouble. I love you." Turning back to Daniel, she says, "Take care. I love you, Little Brother." Then, looking down at Nichole, she says, "I love you too, Squirt." Nichole smiles back at her, rocking left to right, hugging her jar.

Then Daniel tells Nichole, "Now, go clean up your breakfast like I told you." Nichole runs inside. "Be careful!"

Beverly looks at Daniel. "I see she still carrying the jar around with her. You haven't talked to her yet?"

"No, not yet. I will when we get there."

"Okay, Brother, be safe. I love you. Call me if you need me."

Daniel replies, "Love you, too, Sis," as Beverly walks back to her SUV. While she is driving away, Daniel notices Beverly wiping tears from her eyes, and he is reminded of all the pain he and his sister have experienced.

Snapping back from his thoughts, Daniel excitedly says, "Okay, let's get this show on the road." Just then, Michelle walks out, carrying her luggage. "Hey, you just missed Aunt Bev. She said she loves you." Daniel looks at Michelle's luggage. "Do you really need five bags?"

Michelle replies, "Yes, two of them are my shoes."

"You have two bags of just shoes? I don't have enough shoes to even fill up one bag."

She replies, "Maybe you need a fashion lesson, then. All you ever wear are those stupid t-shirts, jeans, and your Converse. That is, when you are not meeting with clients."

"That's true. Sometimes, even with my clients, but I like my t-shirts and jeans. That is just who I am. Maybe I could teach YOU something about fashion."

"I seriously doubt that."

"Hand me your bags, all FIVE of them, and I will pack them in the back. Have you seen your brother?"

At that moment, Niles walks out, wearing his usual headphones with the cord almost dragging the ground and rolling his suitcase behind him. Daniel says to him, "There is Hercules. Little Man got his bag all by himself." An unusual smile appears on Niles's face, and it is not overlooked by Daniel. "Okay, my man, I know your suitcase is packed well because I did it myself. And only ONE pair of shoes, I might add." While loading Nile's suitcase, Daniel looks at Michelle in time to catch a glimpse of her usual response of rolling her eyes to his humor.

The interior of the bus has a fully restored, off-white interior. In the back of the bus is a three-seat bench, where Nathan and Michelle are seated. Behind the driver's seat is a two-seat bench, where Nichole and Niles are buckled in.

Michelle says, whining and looking at the Nissan Armada parked next to the bus in the garage, "Why can't we take the Armada? The seats are sooo much more comfortable."

"Because we are taking the bus." Daniel climbs into the driver's seat and turns to ask, "Okay, has everyone gone to the restroom? Nichole?"

Nathan does not respond. Michelle softly mumbles, "Yes."

Niles nods up and down, and Nichole screams excitedly, "Yes!"

Daniel exclaims, "Okay, then. Away we go!"

Nichole yells out, "Yayyy!" Daniel stops at the stop sign at the intersection at the end of their street, when Nichole suddenly says, "Dad?"

"Yes, Daughter?"

"I need to pee."

Daniel replies, "Seriously?" before making a U-turn back to their home.

AWAKE MY SOUL

Once back on the road, driving down the 10 out of Los Angeles, they pass Exit 22 for Fremont Avenue. Daniel is suddenly taken back in his thoughts to the day he met his wife Emily.

Emily was born and raised in Apalachicola, Florida but is attending college on the west coast. One late-summer night, Daniel is in the front yard of his Kappa Sigma fraternity house. He is teeing off golf balls with some of his fraternity brothers, trying to see how many car alarms they can set off in another fraternity's parking lot during a party being held there. Daniel accidentally slices a shot that lands on the hood of a black Honda Accord passing by. The Honda stops, and a girl with shoulder-length, sandy-blonde hair steps out of the car to check for damage. She shouts, looking at Daniel with her arms raised to her side, "What the hell!"

Daniel calls out to her, "Sorry!" Finding no damage, she gets back into the car, shaking her head in disgust and then driving off quickly.

THE NEXT DAY is the first day of classes for the fall semester. Daniel's fraternity is having an intramural football game later that day against the Pikes. He is wearing his number twenty-two jersey, as well as a pair of sunglasses to hide the evidence of the party the night before. His first class is business law, a class he knows he needs but has dreaded since he got his schedule. Daniel, sitting in the back of the classroom, is watching other students pile in. Suddenly, he sees the girl whose car he hit the night before enter. She takes a seat at the front of the classroom, and Daniel immediately stands, walking over and taking the seat behind her. He could tell she was oblivious of the seat change. That is, until he began tapping her on the shoulder. Not getting her attention, his tapping continues, increasingly harder.

Finally, she turns around, and very abruptly she says, "Okay, enough already. Either you are trying to get my attention, there is something on my shoulder, or you are just annoying. So, which one is it?"

Taken back by her response, Daniel stumbles with his words. "Wow! None. I mean, yes. I mean, no. I mean, I am trying to get your attention, and, apparently, I am annoying, as well."

After an uncomfortable silence, waiting for Daniel to say something, she says, "Well, what do you want, then?"

"Hi, I am Daniel, Daniel White, or apparently Annoying Daniel. And, you are?"

Smiling, she responds, "Hello, Annoying Daniel. My name is Emily Montgomery."

Feeling as if he has secured some sort of victory, Daniel responds, "Hello, Emily."

Looking at him as if she is waiting for him to say something else, she finally speaks up. "So, tell me, Annoying Daniel: Are you expecting a solar flare to come crashing into this classroom? Is that the purpose of the glasses?"

He takes off the sunglasses, and, besides being a little bloodshot, she is taken back by the beauty of his blue eyes. "No. And stop calling me Annoying Daniel."

"You started it."

"Yeah, well, only I can call myself that. Call me by my first name."

Smiling, she says, "I am sorry, Annoying."

"No, just Daniel. Are you always this nice?"

"Sorry. I am only this nice to the third guy that hits on me before ten o'clock each day and hits my car with a golf ball the night before."

"Gotcha. Yeah, sorry about the whole golf-ball thing. I really need to work on my swing."

"You think?"

"Be nice. Just so you won't feel too bad, I hate it when the third guy hits on me before ten o'clock each day, too." Emily laughs. "Well, trying not to sound like I am hitting on you, I have to say I am a little surprised that you have only been hit on three times so far today."

Blushing, smiling, and conceding defeat, Emily breaks eye contact with him, lowering her head. "Thank you, Daniel."

"So, Emily, how would you like to have dinner with me tonight?"

She pauses, mentally processing the request. "I think I

could make that happen, Daniel." She begins writing a note. "Here is my dorm info. What time should I expect you?"

He takes the note from her hand and says, "I will pick you up at seven. Is steak all right?"

"That sounds great."

"I know this incredible upscale restaurant, so you will need to wear something really nice. It's a super fancy place."

She replies, "Will do. By the way, Daniel, twenty-two is my favorite number. If you had been wearing any other jersey, I probably would have blown you off."

The gears turn in his head as he wonders if she is serious or not.

Later that day, during his intramural football game, Daniel injures his left knee. One of his fraternity brothers takes him to the doctor. His leg is placed in a brace, and he is given a pair of crutches. Being stubborn, Daniel does not think he needs them. He gets a ride back to the fraternity house, and he hobbles to his room. He realizes that, with his left leg in a brace, tonight will be a challenge, but he does not want to miss the evening with Emily.

Because of the brace, however, Daniel is stuck wearing shorts. Between that and the x-ray and the doctor visit cutting pretty deeply into his finances, he realizes that the nice restaurant idea has gone out the window.

After an awkward showering event and getting dressed, he climbs into his bus. Moving his seat all the way back, he discovers that, with the brace, his left leg will not fit inside. He rolls down the glass on the driver's side, throws his left leg out the window, closes the door, and departs, receiving quite a few stares while driving around campus with his leg sticking up in the air. Daniel arrives at Emily's dorm, where she is waiting outside. She immediately laughs as he drives up. Daniel had forgotten to inform her about his injury or the change in dinner plans. She is in a nice black dress, and he is in a t-shirt, shorts, and a leg brace.

She speaks first, "Nice bus. Very 1970s."

"Yeah, it needs a little more work, but one day I will have it fully restored."

"You don't look dressed up, and what did you do to your leg?"

"Just a little football injury. The good news is the doctor said I can keep the leg." She laughs, and he continues, "The bad news is we are having dinner at Wendy's instead."

"Wendy's?" She laughs again. "That still sounds okay. Do you think I should change?"

He replies, "No. You look beautiful."

Blushing, she says, "Daniel, no boy has ever made me blush, and you have done it twice in one day. Good job." On the way to the restaurant, she tells him, "I spoke to one of my friends who knows you. She said you are a pretty stand-up guy."

"I am. That is, until I sit down." They both laugh.

At Wendy's, Daniel begins eating his French fries, and she stops him. "No, no, no! You don't use ketchup with fries. You use mayonnaise. Here... Try this." She offers him her cup of mayonnaise, and he dips his fry.

Laughing, Daniel says, "Oh my god. That is amazing. I will never be able to go back to ketchup."

"Daniel, I will tell you something I bet you do not know."

He replies, "Try me."

She tells him, "At the end of last fall, I walked past you when you were dressed in a suit and told you that you looked nice. You totally blew me off. You didn't even say one word."

Shocked, he responds, "What? That was you?"

"Yeah, that was me."

Looking down, he says, "I am so sorry. That was during my hell week, and, as a pledge, I was not allowed to speak to anyone or even get much sleep that week. I hope you will forgive me."

"We'll see. Hell week? What is it? Some kind of cult? You frat boys do strange things."

"No, it's not a cult. It is actually something really special. I would explain it to you, but I don't think there is a way to make anyone who has not gone through it understand."

"Well, going forward, the next time I say something to you, please speak back."

He replies, "Of course, I definitely will. I promise."

She says, "Pinky promise?" He sticks out his little finger and she wraps hers around his, smiling.

He responds, "Pinky promise."

"Okay, I will forgive you then."

Daniel says, "Sorry, we are not eating at a fancy restaurant."

Smiling at Daniel, she says, "You do not need a fancy restaurant. You just need the right company."

"Wise words."

Emily says, "My father taught me that. He taught me a lot."

"Well, I have the right company. I can guarantee you are the best-looking and best-dressed girl to ever eat at a Wendy's." They both laugh. "Say, would you be interested in going to the beach for a bonfire? Some guys from my fraternity all get together every so often and build an amazing bonfire."

She replies, "You had me at beach. Sure, but don't you think I am a little over dressed?"

He says, "I think you look great."

She pauses and replies, "Okay, let's do it, but this time I will drive us. Keys, please?"

He responds, "That is a great idea because I think my leg is still asleep from hanging it out the window."

By the time they reach the bonfire, it is well under way. Emily ditches her shoes in the bus. Stepping out, she says, "I love to feel the sand between my toes."

Mike and Keith, two of Daniel's fraternity brothers, and their girlfriends greet them when they arrive.

Mike says, "Hey, crip. It's about time you showed up."

Daniel, ignoring Mike's comment, says, "Emily, this is Mike and his girlfriend Monica. And this is Keith and Maria."

Emily says, "Hi."

Monica tells Emily, "I love your dress."

Emily replies, "Thank you."

Keith tells them, "Come on and grab a beer."

Mike yells out, "The night is young, and so are we!"

Daniel introduces Emily to the rest of his fraternity brothers and then asks her, "Would you like to take a walk on the beach?"

She replies, "That sounds nice, but how are you going to do that with your knee?"

"Like this." Suddenly, he stands and tosses his crutches onto the fire. Then he takes her hand, helping her up. He limps down toward the waves, never letting go of her. They walk along the shore, looking up at the stars.

Emily says, "I love the ocean so much. The water will always be where my heart is, listening to the waves, feeling the sea breeze, and tasting the salt air on my lips. No matter how far I roam, my heart will always be on the coast. Nothing could be more profoundly perfect for me."

He says, "You definitely sound like a girl who has known the ocean her whole life. So, tell me: Where are you from? There is just a hint of a southern accent I hear. Carolina? Alabama, maybe? No, let me guess: Georgia?"

"Yes, I probably do have a little accent. I'm from the panhandle of Florida - from a little town called Apalachicola, just south of Tallahassee. It is along what we all call the Forgotten Coast."

Daniel responds, "Florida. Cool. Nice beaches down there, I hear."

She asks, "You mean you have never been to Florida?"

"No, but I would like to see it someday."

Again she asks, "You have never even been to Disney World?"

"No. Why go there when we have Disneyland here?"

"True. Well, my parents still live there in Apalachicola, and they also own a beach home on St. George Island."

"An island?" He says. "Nice."

"It is a tiny little island, about twenty minutes from their home in Apalachicola."

"I bet it is nice having a house on the beach."

She responds, "Yeah, it is, but they rent it out most of the time. My father sells real estate."

"That would be a great place to be one. I bet there is a high demand for property down there. So, what brings you to the west coast?"

"Scholarship offers. I had many in state, like Florida, Florida State, Miami, but something drew me here. I guess I just wanted to see the world. What about you? Are you originally from here?"

He replies, "Yep, I was born and raised in Silicon Valley. My dad was into computers early on, and he settled in the Valley. I suppose I am following him in his footsteps."

"So, you are into computers, too?"

"Yeah, pretty much."

She asks, "Do you have any brothers or sisters? I have an older brother and a younger sister."

Daniel replies, "Me too."

"Really?"

"Except I do not have a brother, and my younger sister is older than me." She laughs.

"The stars are so beautiful here, but they do seem prettier back home. Do you ever do much stargazing?" Just then, a shooting star passes in front of them in the night sky. "Wow, did you see that?"

Daniel says, "Yeah, that was a bright one. Yes, I have spent many nights on the beach and have fallen asleep watching the night sky a few times."

"That sounds very peaceful, Daniel. I spent many nights back home doing that but always in a chair, and I never fell asleep. The little crabs always freaked me out when they came out at night. I was always afraid they would get on me if I fell asleep." Daniel works his hand up her arm and along her shoulder, like a spider crawling." She squirms and lets out a fake scream, and they both laugh. Still holding hands, she looks at her watch. "Well, Daniel, as much as I have loved this evening with you, it is getting late, and I have an eight o'clock class tomorrow."

"I understand, Emily."

"I will, however, drive us back. When we get there, are you sure you can drive yourself back to your fraternity house okay?"

"Yes, it is not very far."

THE FOLLOWING EVENING, Daniel shows up at the library for a sociology study group that Emily is in. He arrives there approximately twenty minutes after it starts. Hobbling into the room he says, "Sorry, everyone. I'm late. Do not let me interrupt. Please continue." Emily is surprised to see him. He pulls up a chair behind her.

She whispers to him "What are you doing here?"

"I came here to study."

She asks, "Do you even have sociology?"

"Not this semester, but maybe next." She just gives him that stare - the stare that one day his oldest daughter Michelle would perfect. "Look, I just wanted to see you again. I had the best time of my life last night."

"I did too, Daniel, but how did you know I was here?"

He replies, "I asked around."

"And you don't find that the least bit creepy?"

"No."

"Well, just try and stay quiet. We have our first test tomorrow."

"I promise. Not a word."

Within thirty minutes, Daniel is standing in the center of the group, discussing everything from taking the group through the perspective of sociological imagination to the discussion of micro and macro social construction of reality. At the end of the evening, everyone in the study group is coming up to Daniel and thanking him for the lesson.

Emily walks over to him, laughing, after he shakes the final hand. "What the hell was that?"

"You never asked me what my mother did. She is a sociology teacher. I guess it is kind of ingrained in me. Can I limp you back to your dorm?" he says as he turns toward the door while Emily just laughs and shakes her head, following him.

Walking her back to her dorm, Daniel asks her, "Would you be interested in going out again sometime?"

"Yes, Daniel, I would like that."

He asks, "So, what is it like growing up in Apalachicola?"

"It is about as hometown, apple-pie as you can get. I suppose lots of people would love it. That is pretty evident by all the tourists who visit there every summer. I just feel there is something bigger for me out there. I feel I have some purpose. I guess everybody does, huh?"

"Yeah, Emily, I think you are right."

She asks, "About everyone feeling that way?"

"No, about you having a purpose. I felt it the moment I met you. It is like being around someone really important."

"Thank you, Daniel, I don't think I am really important, but one day... One day, I will leave a lasting impression on many people. I just know it."

THEY SHARE MORE about each other's childhoods while walking, and, just like the night before, Daniel reaches out to hold Emily's hand.

She asks, "You do seem to be hobbling much better today. Are you sure it is okay for you to be doing all this walking on that leg?"

"Yeah, I should be ready for the hundred meters in the Olympics by tomorrow."

She responds, "I doubt that."

"Hey, this boy can dream, right?"

Much sooner than he would have liked, she says, "Well, Daniel, this is my stop."

"So, do you have a street view from your room?"

With a look of concern on her face, she asks, "Yeah. Why? Tell me you are not going to pull one of those John Cusack moments, standing out here with a boombox on your head, playing Peter Gabriel."

"Well, now I'm not. Thanks for blowing it." They both laugh.

"No, I was just wondering which room was yours."

"Mine is the third window from the left on the second floor. In fact, it's a little embarrassing, but if you look hard enough you can see one of my bras hanging from the curtain rod, drying."

"Oh, nice. Yes, I see it. And I was thinking that was some new European designer drapes."

Laughing, she tells him, "Okay, Daniel, I need to go. They give us a midnight curfew."

"Yeah, I wouldn't want you to miss that. I will see you tomorrow morning, then, in class."

"Yes. Thank you for hobbling me home. See you tomorrow, Daniel."

"Goodnight, Emily."

"Goodnight, Daniel."

Walking away, Daniel begins loudly singing Peter

Gabriel's song *In Your Eyes* so she can hear him. Emily laughs at him all the way to her door.

After a couple more weeks of dinner dates at Wendy's and In and Out, late one Friday night, shortly before curfew, Daniel shows up outside Emily's dorm. Walking better now, however still wearing his leg brace, Daniel stands below her window holding a handful of dime-size rocks he gathered along the way there. He begins throwing them at her window. First one hits. Second one hits. Third one misses. Fourth one hits Emily directly in the eye as she opens her window. He is certain anyone from the dorm across the street can hear her as she yells. "Ow! Shit! What the hell?"

Daniel panics. He begins spinning completely around, pivoting on his good leg. Trying to run in three different directions at once, Daniel does not know whether to stay or leave. He thinks to himself, "Maybe she did not see me. Maybe she will think a squirrel threw an acorn at her. Wait, squirrels cannot throw things. Maybe..."

After a moment, while standing there upset and wondering what to do, with both of his hands pulling on his hair, Emily walks out crying.

She says, "What are you doing?"

"Oh my god. I was just trying to get your attention."

"Well, you got it! Have you ever heard of calling someone? Damn it. I think I need to go to the hospital."

Still panic stricken, Daniel says, "Let me run and get my bus."

"You fool, you cannot run on your hurt leg."

He nervously exclaims, "You are right."

She says, "We will have to take my car. You will have to drive, though."

Hurriedly, he says, "Okay. I got this. Let's go!"

Daniel drove Emily to the hospital, something he would not do again until the birth of their first child, Michelle. Cars were pulling over to let the Honda Accord pass, with its emergency flashers on, Daniel's leg sticking out the window into the night sky, and Emily yelling at him the entire way. A security guard sees them pulling up to the emergency room. Between Daniel's leg being up in the air and Emily yelling at him while holding her eye in pain, he says, "College kids," shaking his head.

Daniel waits in the lobby. When Emily finally comes out, he asks, "How are you?"

"The doctor said I was lucky, and I should have full vision tomorrow."

"I am so sorry. I was just trying to get you to the window."

"Well, it worked!"

"Luckily, you were... seen quickly." Daniel says, and he laughs with no response from Emily other than the stare. "Get it? Seen? Your eye?" Still, only the stare.

After leaving the hospital, they grab some food at In and Out before heading back to campus. Once back to her dorm, with Emily holding a bandage over her eye, Daniel asks, "Will you get in trouble for being late getting back?"

"No, I have the paperwork from the emergency room."

He asks, "Are you doing anything tomorrow?"

"No."

"Would you like to... see me?" He chuckles, and she punches his chest. "Ow..."

Laughing, she says, "Yes, I would."

"I will pick you up around noon. There is place I would like to show you. It will be an all-day trip. I think you will like what you... see."

"Stop it!"

"Sorry. Sorry about everything."

"I will forgive you this time. Goodnight, Daniel."

"Goodnight, Emily. I will... see you tomorrow." They both smile.

Saturday afternoon arrives, and Daniel shows up to pick her up for the first time without a leg brace. As she gets in the bus, he looks at her right eye, which is still bloodshot. He asks, "How is your eye?"

"Let's just say, I am seeing red, so no seeing-eye jokes. Deal?"

"Deal."

She says, "Glad to see your leg is better."

"You did that one, not me." She pushes his shoulder. "Me too. I had forgotten what it is like driving with my leg actually in a vehicle."

After a five-hour drive on scenic Highway 1 along the Pacific, they arrive at their destination near sunset.

"This beach is called Glass Beach."

She asks, "Why is it called Glass Beach. Is there sea glass here?"

"You might say that. My parents used to bring me here when I was a child."

Stepping out of the bus and walking down to the water, Emily says, "Oh my god. This is so beautiful. It is so hard to find sea glass back home. Here, it is everywhere."

Daniel says, "This use to be a dump back in the early

part of the twentieth century. People threw all their garbage into the sea. The ocean had other ideas and gave it back to us this way. It used to be so much prettier, but people kept walking away with bags of glass pebbles."

"Daniel, it is still so beautiful here. I can only imagine what it looked like before. Thank you for sharing it with me."

"You're welcome, Emily."

While walking along the beach and holding hands, they witnessed their first sunset together.

"Wow, Emily, I have seen many sunsets on the water, but there is something about this one I know I will never forget."

Emily says, "It is so beautiful. I can never see enough sunrises and sunsets over the ocean."

Daniel asks her, "So, who is your favorite poet?"

"That would have to be Keats."

He says, "Keats. Good choice. 'O that our dreamings all, of sleep or wake, Would all their colours from the sunset take.'"

She replies, "'From something of material sublime, Rather than shadow our own soul's day-time In the dark void of night.'"

"Very nice, Emily."

"You too, Daniel. You know your Keats."

"As do you. Emily, I have never felt like I do when I am with you. It is as if the world has stopped and is waiting on you to make it move."

After a long stretch of silence, she says, "Daniel?"

"Yes, Emily?" She stops walking, staring into his eyes.

"Daniel, do not fall for me. I do not want my life to be planned. I don't know what I will be doing, who I will be, or where I will be tomorrow. Daniel, do not fall for me. I do not think you, or anyone else, is ready for someone like me at this time in my life. Do not fall for me because, if you do, I don't think I could keep from falling for you, too."

At that moment, Daniel says, "It is too late, Emily. I already have." His right hand touches her cheek, and he kisses her for the first time.

Following the sunset, they stop and eat at Mendo Bistro in the nearby town of Fort Bragg, California before the long drive back home that, for both of them, could not be long enough. After that moment on the beach, all they wanted was to be with each other for the rest of their lives.

Daniel was beginning to recall the night Emily sneaked him, wearing a wig and a dress, into her dorm, when suddenly he is swept out of his daydream by the voice of his oldest daughter, "Dad?"

"Daughter?"

Michelle says, "I need a restroom stop."

"Can it wait a few more miles? I would like us to get farther out away from all the congestion before we have to stop."

Michelle whispers something to Nichole in front of her. Nichole then leans up and whispers into Daniel's ear.

Immediately, he slams on the brakes and crosses two lanes of traffic to take an exit. Daniel pulls up to the first convenience store he finds and parks. Michelle steps out of the bus, telling him, "I am going to the restroom. Please buy me something and send it with Nichole to me."

Daniel tells Niles, "Hey, buddy, stay in here with Nathan. I will be right back. Come on, Nichole." Daniel quickly walks into the store.

Following him, Nichole calls out, "Wait!" She runs back to the bus to grab her jar and then joins Daniel inside.

Nichole is drawn to the candy aisle, and she asks, "Dad?"

"Daughter?"

"Why don't they stock candy on every shelf?"

"Some people think other foods are good besides just candy."

She says, "Well, they are wrong."

Daniel finds the menstrual-hygiene product section. Frustrated and confused, he says, "There are like a hundred different kinds. How am I supposed to know what to get?"

Nichole takes a box off the shelf, and says, "Dad, it's okay. Here, this one will work."

"Awesome, sweetheart. Thank you."

As he is paying the store clerk, Michelle storms in, saying, "What is taking you so long?"

Nichole says, "I wish I could get my period."

Michelle and the clerk look at her and say in unison, "No, you don't." Michelle takes the box from Daniel's hands and walks out.

The clerk looks at Daniel and says, "Always remember: They need their parents, even if they do not always show it."

"I hope you are right. Thanks. Come on, Nichole. Let's

get back to the bus." Daniel meets Michelle coming out of the restroom and says to her, "This is your first one. Do you want to call Aunt Bev and ask any advice?"

Michelle gives him that stare and says, "Dad, I have Google."

Climbing back into the bus, he sarcastically replies, "Yeah, Google. I forgot. I know that is where I turn for life-changing advice. Okay, is everybody ready? Here we go."

While they are waiting to pull out into traffic, Nichole says, "Dad?"

Knowing what she is about to say, he turns the wheel back to the parking spot he just left.

She says, "I am sorry. I will hurry. I promise." She looks at Michelle. "Will you please go with me? Please?" Michelle rolls her eyes and follows her to the restroom.

A LITTLE FAIRY DUST

Once back on the road and driving through the desert, Daniel is reminded of his and Emily's wedding and all that led up to it.

It is the end of May in 2001, and Daniel and Emily are not only are graduating, but they also are making plans for their summer wedding. Emily has her hands full sending out graduation and wedding announcements when suddenly everything changes. Following the graduation ceremony, Daniel's father, who is a licensed pilot, is flying to Sonoma with Daniel's mother in their private Cessna. They invite Daniel and Emily to join them for the weekend. The two consider the offer; however, they decline. The following morning, Daniel receives a phone call from his sister Beverly. Daniel's father's plane went down shortly after takeoff, and neither of his parents survived.

Emily tries her hardest to comfort Daniel. He is dealing with not only with the grief of losing his parents but also with the psychological effect of knowing how close he and Emily came to being on that plane. Their wedding is planned, and invitations have been sent, but Emily feels it would be better to elope, even against her mother's wishes. Emily knows how difficult it would be for Daniel to have a formal wedding so soon without his mom and dad. They decide to elope to Las Vegas - a decision that disappointed Emily's mom for many years. On their way to Las Vegas, driving through the desert, Daniel's alternator goes out on his bus, leaving them stranded on the shoulder.

Emily asks, "What are we going to do?" Checking her phone, she says, "There is no phone signal out here, and who the hell knows how far the next town is."

Stepping out of the bus, Daniel replies, "I will try and wave down someone to help us." After several cars pass without stopping, Daniel says, "Maybe you can have better luck than me."

Emily stands on the shoulder, trying to flag cars down for assistance. When one finally slows down, they speed back up when they see Daniel. Emily calls out to Daniel, who is now sitting on the ground. "I think if it were two women broken down, people might stop!"

Daniel, with a look of concern, says in defiance, "I know what you are thinking. No, no, no, no!"

"Come on! It worked in college, getting you into my dorm. Why would it not work now?"

"Because, I am not going to dress up like a woman again. Ever! That was not the proudest moment of my life."

Smiling, using her irresistible charm, Emily says, "So maybe it wasn't your proudest moment, but it was definitely the luckiest night of your life. Come on. It's hot out here. I am hungry and thirsty."

"You just like seeing me in a dress."

"Please? For your future bride. Please...?"

"All right. What do I have to put on?"

Emily replies, "I have just the perfect thing for you to wear." Smiling, she pulls out her wedding dress.

"No. Are you serious?"

"Yes, it will fit you perfectly."

He says, "I think there must be some dark, sadistic side to you."

Emily helps Daniel into her wedding dress. Looking down, Daniel says, "I am a little flat chested, don't you think?"

"You're right. You definitely need some boobs." Rummaging through her suitcase, she says, "Here is one of my bras. Just put it on over your t-shirt."

"Why over my t-shirt?"

Emily replies, "So none of your chest hairs will poke out. Here... Stuff it with your socks from your suitcase."

"Really? I cannot believe I am freaking doing this again."

She says, "Oh, shut up. You look great." Handing him her veil, she adds, "Here, put this on."

"I am not wearing a freaking veil. This is bad enough."

She pleads, saying, "Come on. I am thirsty. You need to hide your head."

"Because of shame?"

"No, stupid. Because you have a goatee and short hair."

"Good point."

She tells him, "Your jeans need to come off, too. I can see them at the base of the dress."

As he pulls off his jeans from underneath the dress, Daniel says, "This is so freaking embarrassing."

"Okay, here, put my heels on."

"Seriously?"

"Yes. You have to make this believable, or we will be out here all day."

Putting them on, he says, "They don't even fit. Look my heel hangs off the back of them."

Emily tells him, "Just deal with it. You don't have to wear them very long."

Once he is dressed, they both stand behind the bus waving, and immediately someone stops. It is an old beat-up truck driven by an extremely hairy man, wearing coveralls and no undershirt.

Emily says, "I told you it would work."

The driver asks them, "You girls need a ride?"

Emily does all the talking so Daniel's voice doesn't give their plan away. "Yes. My friend here is getting married, and our bus broke down on the way to Vegas."

He says, "Hop on in, and I will take you to the next town."

She replies, "Thanks." Emily makes Daniel get in first so he can sit next to the driver.

As he drives away, he tells them, "My name is Billy."

"Hello, Billy. My name is Emily, and this is my friend Danielle." Daniel, keeping the veil down, looks to his right at Emily, scowling.

Billy asks, "So you're getting hitched, huh?"

Daniel answers with as high of a pitch as he can muster, while Emily keeps giggling. "Uh huh."

Emily is having a blast. She sees a billboard sign showing only one more mile to the next town and decides to get Daniel one more time. Emily says, "Yeah, Danielle here was supposed to have a male stripper at her bachelorette party last night, but he didn't show. Yep, all she wanted was just one more fling before tying the knot." Emily starts laughing again, while Daniel is staring at her through the veil. "If we just could find her someone to rock her world just one more time."

Billy laughs. Smiling, he looks at Daniel, and he places a hand on Daniel's knee. Suddenly, Daniel strips off his veil, exposing his face, and looks at Emily, yelling, "Come on, seriously!"

"What the hell!" Billy yells and swerves into oncoming traffic, practically throwing Daniel into his lap. Then, he swerves back to the right lane before pulling over to the shoulder. "Get out, both of you freaks! You people belong in Vegas! Men wearing dresses... What the hell is this world coming to?" The two of them get out of his truck, and he spins his tires as he drives off. Luckily, they were only a hundred yards from the town.

Emily is laughing so hard; she is literally rolling around on the ground. She looks up at Daniel who is fuming in her dress and says. "I'm sorry. Oh my god! I am so sorry! That was so much fun! Your face..."

Daniel is beginning to calm down, and he helps her up off the ground. Going to hug him, she says, "I'm so sorry, Danielle." Daniel drops her back on the ground, where she starts rolling and laughing again. "Just one more fling..."

After Daniel calms down again and Emily collects herself, they walk to the service station with Daniel still in the dress.

ARCTURUS

Daniel is laughing to himself, driving on the 40 just a few miles east of Ludlow, California in the Mojave Desert, when the bus begins slowing to a crawl. He coasts to the right shoulder and parks.

He says, "You have got to be kidding me! Great! Talk about timing."

Nichole asks, "Dad, what's wrong?"

Michelle says, "I told you we should have taken the Armada."

Daniel replies, as they come to a stop, "We just have a little engine trouble. I'm going to get out and take a look at it. Everyone stay in the bus." Daniel exits the driver's side, walking to the rear of the bus. He unhooks his bike and removes the bike carrier clamped on the tailgate to gain access to the engine. While leaning over, he looks to his right, and Nichole is standing right next to him, also looking as if she knew something about vehicle maintenance. He tells her, "I thought I told you to stay in the bus."

She smiles and says, "Well, I thought you might need some help."

Daniel mumbles, "Let's see. We are about forty miles away from the next town. The last town was about ten miles back." He glances at his cell phone. "And I have no signal." Then, he looks down at Nichole and asks, "Your sister doesn't have a dress, does she?" Nichole looks at Daniel, confused. "Never mind."

Nichole asks, "What's wrong?"

He replies, "With the bus?" She nods yes. "I am not sure. It looks like everything is fine. It's too soon for it to be the alternator or the battery. I just replaced them both a few months ago." Daniel starts stroking his chin while thinking. When he looks to his right, he sees Nichole and now Niles are standing there and stroking their chins, as well.

Nichole says, "You always have your mountain bike. Why don't you just ride it to get help?"

Daniel leans over again, looking at the engine, and says, "I'm not riding a bike through the desert." Niles begins pulling on Daniel's jeans. He turns to him, frustrated. "What is it Niles?" Daniel looks behind them in the direction Niles is pointing.

Nichole is pointing, as well, and says, "Well, he is."

Coming up on the shoulder of the road is a little man with a long grey beard and long grey hair riding on a squeaky, three-wheel bike pulling a cart. He is wearing a black top hat with long feathers sticking out of it. He has tiny, round, wire-rimmed glasses and is wearing a white ruffled shirt covered by what appears to be a long red waistcoat. The coat easily could have been taken from George Harrison on the cover of the Beatles' Sergeant Pepper album. He is also wearing green tights and shiny black boots. Pedaling slowly, he stops behind the bus. He steps off the bike, and they discover that he is barely under five feet tall.

Nichole says, pointing at him, "You are short." Daniel nudges her to correct her manners.

Smiling at her, the little man says to Nichole, "My dear, you are shorter than I, so that makes me tall. Hello, my name is Atticus Ceffyl-Dwr Hampelman, Fairy and Wish-Maker Extraordinaire."

Nichole, giggling, says, "Hello, Atticus C...Cif... I cannot remember the rest."

"No worries, my dear. Looks like you folks are having a little mechanical distress."

Daniel replies, "Yeah, I cannot, for the life of me, figure out what is wrong."

Atticus says, "This is a nice vehicle. I know a little bit about transports. I do not own one myself and never have, but, if you do not mind, I can give it a little look over."

Daniel is thinking to himself, "This guy is a few bricks short of a load and is probably wasting his time. I have worked on this bus for over twenty years, and he calls it a transport. But, since I have no clue what is wrong, I might as well let him try." He says, "Absolutely, Atticus Have at it."

Michelle and Nathan get out of the bus to admire their new friend, as Niles with his headphones on continues to stare at Atticus in amazement.

While Atticus is looking at the engine, he keeps mumbling out loud, moving his head up and down like a parrot. "Hmmm... Yes... Oh, yes.... No... Ah ha!... No... Hmmm..."

Daniel says, "I replaced the alternator and the battery a couple of months ago, so it shouldn't be that."

Atticus replies, "I see. Hmmm..."

Nichole asks, "Why are you so short? You're like an elf." Daniel nudges her again, shaking his head no.

Atticus laughs at her and says, "Elves aren't real my child. Just ask any other fairy, and they will tell you the same thing."

Smiling, Nichole replies, "I like you."

Atticus, laughing, asks her, "Would you mind, my dear, going to my cart and fetching me the burgundy-colored wand in my bag - the one with the glass bead embedded in the handle?" Daniel is becoming reassured that his first impression of Atticus was correct.

Nichole reaches into his bag and pulls out a wand. She takes it to him and says, "Here you go, Atticus."

Atticus reaches over his shoulder, taking the wand. "Oh no, dear, that is not the right one. You cannot fix a combustion engine with that wand. Bring me the one to the left of it. Burgundy, my dear. Burgundy!" She returns to his cart, and Atticus shakes his head, laughing. Looking up at Daniel, he tells him, "These kids these days... You send them for a dragon-tooth wand, and they bring you a feather-pear wand instead."

Daniel uneasily laughs with him on the outside but is getting more and more concerned with Atticus's sanity on the inside. "Yes, these kids and their feather-pear wands, I tell you."

Nichole returns with another wand, and Atticus tells her, "Oh, yes... yes. Now that is the right wand." Nichole smiles. He leans back over the engine while Daniel is holding his finger over his lips looking at Nichole because he knows she is about to say something else that she shouldn't. "Yes. Oh, yes... Just like I suspected!"

Daniel anxiously asks, "What? What is it?"

Atticus replies, "Somewhere during my journey today, I lost a bead from my hair. Yes, right there."

Daniel is thinking, "And you lost some marbles from your head, as well. I cannot believe I am standing here in the desert with a person working on my bus with a freaking wand. Emily would love this."

Nichole asks Atticus, "If I rub your belly while there is a rainbow, would I get three wishes?"

Atticus looks at her with a look of confusion on his face, saying, "Young lady, I am not Buddha, a genie, or a leprechaun. By the way, genies are not real, either, and the only place you will see a leprechaun is on a cereal box, my dear." Atticus notices Nichole sadly lowering her head. "If you did have a wish, little girl, what would you wish for?"

Nichole says, "I would wish for my mom to come back."

Atticus begins looking all around, asking, "Where did she go?"

Holding up her jar, Nichole says, "She's in here. She died."

Atticus lowers his head saying, "Oh... Hmm... I see."

She adds, "I would also wish that I had everything, so then I would not need any more wishes."

Atticus tells her, "I see. I lost my dear mum a long, long time ago. In fact, she gave me this." He searches through his coat pockets. "No, that's not it. Maybe this pocket... No... Hmmm... Ah, there it is. She gave me this." Atticus pulls out a small pewter fairy figurine, approximately three inches tall. The fairy figurine has her ankles crossed with her arms and wings spread wide. In her hand is a little wand with a tiny gem at the point.

Nichole calls out, "It looks like Tinker Bell!"

Atticus asks, "Who? Never mind. Besides being a very good luck charm, my dear, my mum told me that if I held it against my heart and closed my eyes while thinking of her, she would appear. But, you have to keep your eyes closed, or she will disappear again. Here, you try it." Atticus hands it to her. "Oh, and think of your mum, not mine." He chuckles.

Nichole says, "It works! It works! I see my mommy."

He tells her, "You keep that, and, whenever you miss her, just do what I told you."

Nichole looks sad again, trying to hand it back to Atticus. "But, if I take it, you will not be able to see your mom anymore."

Atticus says, patting his pockets, "I think I have another one lying around here somewhere. You keep it, my dear."

"Thank you, Atticus." She hugs his neck, and he laughs.

Nichole walks over to show it to her sister, and Atticus looks up at Daniel, while winking, whispering loudly, and laughing, "The power of suggestion..."

Daniel looks at Atticus and smiles, saying, "Thank you."

Then, Atticus asks, "What might your chronometer display?"

Daniel replies, "My what?" Atticus points to Daniel's wrist. "Oh, my watch? It's a quarter after two."

Atticus responds, "Excellent. Excellent." Then, suddenly, he calls out, and everyone jumps. "All right! Now go into the transport, place your metal scepter into the ignitor aperture, and rotate it."

Daniel says, laughing, "Okay, you mean try to start it?"

Atticus, looking confused, responds, "Why yes...Yes, that is what I said."

Daniel laughs again, climbing into the bus. He turns the key, and, to his surprise, it starts immediately. "Well, I'll be damned."

Nichole screams, "Yay! Atticus, you did it!"

Daniel, climbing out of the driver's seat, is thinking to himself, "I'm sure the bus just needed to rest. I don't believe Atticus had anything to do with it starting, but what he did for Nichole... That was real magic."

He goes back to Atticus and asks him, "What did you do, my friend?"

"Oh, it is too complicated for me to explain. It took me a couple hundred years to perfect it."

Overlooking Atticus's mental stability, Daniel has

grown quite fond of him, and he shakes his hand. "Thank you so much, Atticus. Can I pay you something for your trouble?" Daniel reaches for his wallet.

Atticus replies, "No... No... No trouble. It was no trouble at all."

Daniel asks, "Can we offer you a ride, perhaps?"

"Oh, no. No thank you. I can go much faster on my bike." Again, Daniel is surprised that he is so entertained at the conversation he is having with Atticus. "I will be on my way, folks. You all have a good day." Then, he leans over to Nichole and Niles and says, "Now, you two make sure you tell everyone you know that elves are not real. If no one believes you, tell them a fairy told you." Then, he winks and climbs on his bike. Tipping his hat to them, he passes the bus, riding away on the shoulder.

Nichole yells out, "Goodbye, Atticus!" Atticus honks the horn on his bike as a reply.

Daniel checks the engine again, and it all looks great. "Okay, folks, I don't know what just happened, but we have lost almost an hour, so let's get back on the road."

THEY ALL CLIMB into the bus, continuing their journey. Twenty-five miles down the road, Nichole asks Daniel, "Dad?"

"Yes, Daughter?"

"What happened to Atticus?" At that moment, Daniel looks at the speedometer that shows him going sixty-five miles per hour. He realizes they have not passed Atticus in either direction.

"Yeah, where did he go?" Michelle points out, "We haven't passed any towns or roads."

Then Nathan, who has remained to himself most of the

trip says, "There has been nothing but desert, and I could walk faster backwards than Santa's helper was peddling."

Nichole yells out, "He's not an elf! He's a fairy."

Daniel is at a loss for words, thinking to himself, "Someone must have given him a ride." Up ahead, he sees flashing lights. Slowing down, he discovers there has been an accident with a car and a tractor trailer. They pass a state police officer, who is waving traffic though. In the back of his mind, he cannot help but wonder if perhaps there was a reason for the breakdown after all. Daniel says softly out loud, "Thanks again, Atticus."

A GRAND VIEW

DANIEL and his family finally arrive at the South Rim of the Grand Canyon just before dusk. Daniel secures their campsite at Mather Campground and begins unloading the tent. He asks Niles, "Hey buddy, you want to give me a hand?" Niles nods yes.

Daniel is struggling to set up the tent while Niles is looking at the instruction book. Suddenly, Niles stands, taking the tent rods out of Daniel's hands, and within two minutes shows him how to set the tent up. Laughing, Daniel says, "I guess that is what they mean when they say it is so easy a five year old can do it."

After the long drive and setting up their campsite, everyone is exhausted and ready to turn in for the night – everyone, that is, except for Michelle. "Oh my god, Dad! I cannot get any cell service here. Holy crap! What am I going to do?"

Daniel responds, "Here is a novel idea: Maybe you should try and go a couple of days without the internet. I heard, and it may just be a rumor, but I was told there was once a time long ago when people actually spoke to one another in person, and there were no such things as cell phones."

Michelle, in frustration, responds, "There was also a time when people stopped sleeping in the outdoors and started staying in houses and hotels."

"Yeah, yeah, yeah. Hey, has anyone seen Nathan?"

Michelle replies, "Yeah, he said he was going for a walk."

After approximately thirty minutes, Nathan returns to the campsite. Daniel says, "Nichole, you and your sister grab the sleeping bags and the overnight bags from the bus. Nathan give them a hand."

Michelle says, "I want to sleep in the bus instead of the tent."

Nichole then says, "Me too. But, Dad, you still need to spray the monster spray. You didn't forget it did you?"

Daniel replies, "No, I did not forget it." Ever since the children were little, Daniel and Emily would spray a bottle of lavender essential oil, labeled monster spray. It was to keep all the monsters away while they slept. "All right. Nathan, can you grab three sleeping bags from the bus while I spray the monster spray?" Nathan nods yes. "Thank you, sir."

AFTER STARGAZING FOR A WHILE, Daniel joins Nathan and Niles in the tent. Within twenty minutes, the coyotes begin howling, and Michelle and Nichole run from the bus to the tent, carrying their sleeping bags.

Entering the tent, Michelle says, "We decided we would rather sleep in the tent tonight."

Laughing, Daniel says, "Okay, just zip it up - the tent and your mouth, Nichole."

She reluctantly responds, "All right."

Daniel says, "Goodnight, everyone."

The girls and Nathan reply in unison, "Goodnight."

Nichole says, "Dad?"

"Daughter?"

"Will you walk me to the restroom?"

Michelle says, "Good Lord, I told you to go before we went to sleep. Dad, do you want me to take her?"

Daniel replies, "No, I have it. Come on, Nichole."

Walking out, Nichole says, "Sorry, Dad. Thank you."

He replies, "No worries, Sweetie."

On their way to the restroom, Nichole asks, "Dad, would a coyote eat me?"

Daniel replies, "Perhaps, but not with me here."

Nichole asks, "Are you not scared of them?"

"No. Honestly, I think they are more scared of us, with good reason."

She asks, "What do you mean?"

"Well, a lot of people, far too many actually, are not very nice to animals."

Nichole says, "That makes me sad. Some animals aren't nice to other animals either. Just look at how Road Runner tricks Coyote all the time. But, Coyote isn't always nice to Road Runner either. I think he wants to eat him. Dad, what were you looking for in the sky earlier?"

Daniel replies, "I was just looking at the stars."

"Mom used to do that a lot, too." Nichole said, as she turned her eyes to the sky.

Looking up, he says, "Yes, she did. It's quite a grand view, isn't it?"

Nichole responds, "Yes, it is." Spotting a falling star, she says, "Dad! Did you see that?"

"Yes, that was a good one. Make a wish."

Pausing for a moment, she says, "Okay, I made it. Do you want to know what it is?"

Daniel tells her, "No. You should never tell your wish, or it won't come true."

"Okay, I can keep a secret, as long as it is only to myself."

"That means you can't even tell your imaginary friend."

"Dad, I am a big girl now. I don't have imaginary friends anymore. Besides, they weren't my imaginary friends. I was theirs." Daniel laughs. "Did you make a wish?" She asks.

"Yes, I did."

Nichole says, "Well, don't tell me, or it will not come true."

Patting her shoulder, Daniel tells her, "Okay, I won't tell."

THE NEXT MORNING, Daniel was up early with Nichole and Niles. Daniel says, "I don't know what it is, but suddenly when kids become teenagers, they sleep half their days away. But, you want to know how to wake up a teenager?"

Nichole asks, "How? Do you throw cold water on them? Do you rub your slippers on the carpet and shock them? Pop a balloon? Scream? I know... Shoot them in the face with a rubber band?"

Daniel says, "Seriously? I'm glad you weren't my sister. No. You say, 'Who is ready for some breakfast?'" Suddenly, Michelle and Nathan stumble out of the tent like hibernating bears with the arrival of spring, rubbing their eyes. "You guys get dressed, and we will go grab some food and look around."

AFTER BREAKFAST at the Bright Angel restaurant, they take in the view of the Grand Canyon from the observation overlook. Then, everyone fills their backpacks with water and food, and Nichole makes sure to pack her jar. Daniel leads them out for a day hike on Bright Angel Trail.

On the way to the trail, Michelle sees the Bright Angel Lodge and asks, "Dad, can we stay there tonight?"

Daniel answers, "No."

Michelle replies, "I don't want to camp again."

Daniel asks his group, "Okay, did everyone pack their lunches and lots of water? During the summer, temperatures can reach above a hundred and twenty degrees.

Nichole and Michelle answer, "Yes." Niles shakes his head.

Daniel looks over to Nathan waiting on a response, "Nathan?"

Nathan says, "Yes, sir."

Reaching the trailhead, Nichole reads a sign out loud. "This sign says, 'Warning. DO NOT attempt to hike from canyon rim to river and back in one day. Each year hikers suffer serious illness or death from exhaustion.' Holy smoke, Dad! It says we could die."

Daniel tells them, "It is important that you stay with me, and - Nichole especially - it is important that you listen to what I say. You have to be respectful to Mother Nature. Hiking is very dangerous. It is not Disneyland out here. The drop offs are real, the heat is real, and the snakes are real."

Michelle says, "Snakes!"

Daniel says, "Okay, if everyone is ready, let's go."

Right away, they see the first tunnel that is cut into the rock wall. Nichole calls out, "Dad, look there is a tunnel. We get to go through it."

Daniel says, "Yes, we do. There is another one farther ahead. This valley off to our right is called the Canyon's bathtub ring."

Nichole asks, "Why is it called a bathtub ring?"

Daniel says, "If you look down at it from the rim, the rock layers look like a ring around a bathtub. I will show you when we get back up."

Nathan points out, "Hey, look! There is graffiti on the wall up there."

Daniel says, "That's not graffiti. Well, I suppose you can say it is very old graffiti. Those are called petroglyphs. They are markings made over a thousand years ago."

Nichole says, "Dad that is impossible. Columbus didn't discover North America until 1492."

Daniel says, "He actually didn't discover North America at all, but that is another story. If he had, which he didn't, who would Columbus supposedly have met?"

She replies, "Indians?"

Daniel says, "That's right: Indians who were here long before anyone else."

Michelle asks, "How long is this hike going to be?"

Daniel tells her, "It is about four and a half miles and a little over three thousand feet down. Then it's another four and a half miles and a little over three thousand feet back up."

Michelle replies, "Dad, that is nine miles. That is more than I walk in a month."

Daniel says, "Good math skills. Well, it will be good for you then."

Michelle says, "Dad, I don't want to hike that far."

Daniel tells her, "We are hiking down to the Indian Garden. There is a Starbucks there."

Michelle says, "All right, then. I can do it for Starbucks."

Nichole asks Daniel, "Dad, why is it called Indian Garden?"

Daniel answers, "Indian Garden is a campground where there is a small oasis. The Garden Creek there runs year-round. It got its name because the Indians used to raise crops there, like squash and corn, and the trail we are taking was the same one the Indians used to get there." A group of hikers are heading back up, and Daniel tells the kids, "Hey guys, always give the uphill hikers the right of way."

FARTHER DOWN, almost a mile and a half in, Nichole says, "Dad?"

"Daughter?"

"I need a restroom."

Daniel replies, "Okay, hold it a little longer. Right up here is our first rest stop."

Michelle says, "This is not as bad as I thought it would be."

THEY ARRIVE at the first Rest House at the mile and a half marker. There are two Rest Houses along the way to Indian Gardens. The second Rest House is at the three-mile marker. The Rest Houses are rock formations with stacked stones covered by a man-made roof.

At the Rest House, Michelle asks Daniel, "Dad?"

"Daughter?"

"Can I talk to you about something?" She looks around at everyone. "In private?"

Daniel says, "Sure. Let's go over here."

Finding a nice spot by a boulder she tells him, "Dad there is a boy I like a lot. How did you know mom was the one for you?"

Daniel replies, "Well, first of all, you are still too young to be worried about the one. There is still lots of time for that. Think of it as shoes. You like shoes. I know because you brought a thousand pairs with us. You don't just walk into a shoe store grab a pair and walk out. You have to try on many pairs until you find the right fit."

She responds, "I get that, but how did you know? You know, with Mom?"

He says, "That's a tough one. It could have been when I saw her the first time and she yelled at me for hitting her car with a golf ball, or I could say it was when I was so persistent to get her attention in class that she called me annoying, but I think it was when we walked on the beach together the first time. That night, she opened up to me. At that moment, I felt she was telling me things that she had never been comfortable enough to tell anyone else. I think love is about being so comfortable with someone that you can expose your soul, your dreams, and your desires to them - and them to you. You both feel safe."

Michelle says, "You're right. I am nowhere near that level yet. So, I'm not saying he is the one, but I really like him. With school starting back soon, I don't know what to expect."

Daniel asks, "What do you mean?"

"Well, like I said, I really like him, and he seems to really like me except for when his friends are around. I guess I am not in his circle. I think he wants me to be like them."

Daniel says, "I see. Well, the key is to always be yourself. If someone does not like you for who you are - if they want you to be someone who you aren't - then they never really liked you anyway."

"It just makes me sad."

He responds, "That is the first warning sign. You want to make sure you are just as happy alone as you are when you are with someone. Never let how someone feels about you, whether they like you or not, make or break you."

Michelle says, "Thanks, Dad."

She walks over, joining the others, and Daniel looks up and says out loud softly, "How was that, Em?"

THREE MILES LATER, they finally arrive at their destination: The Indian Garden campground. Staking a claim on one of the picnic tables, Michelle says, "Dad, I see no Starbucks here."

Daniel says, "They must have closed it."

Michelle replies, "There never was one, was there?"

Daniel admits, "No, but would you have trekked all this way if you knew the truth?"

She says, "No. I probably wouldn't have."

Beginning to eat their lunch, Nichole asks, "Dad, when you came here, was mom with you?"

Daniel answers, "Yep, except we hiked a lot farther down. We went about another five miles and stayed in a cabin at Phantom Ranch."

Nichole asks, "Phantom Ranch? That sounds scary. Can we go there and spend the night?"

Michelle says, "No. We are not going any farther into this giant hole in the ground."

Daniel answers Nichole, "No, you have to make reservations over a year in advance. The lodge fills up quickly. The only reason your mom and I got to stay there was because a friend of hers had to cancel. They gave us their reservation."

Nichole asks, "What is it like?"

Daniel replies, "It's really nice. There are beautiful rock cabins, a restaurant, and a beach on the Colorado river."

Nichole says, "A beach?"

Michelle says, "If you tell me there is a Starbucks, I will not believe you."

Daniel says, "No Starbucks. There are shade trees that line the creek. It is really a beautiful place."

Nichole asks, "Dad, can we drink from the creek here?"

Daniel says, "No. You should never drink from creeks or rivers. There is a water source here like the one at the mile and a half Rest House. You can fill your water there."

Nichole says, "Dad, I wish we could camp here."

Michelle says, "Shut up."

Nichole says, "I was telling Dad, not you. You are not the boss."

Daniel says, "You two, try and get along. I wanted to, but they were filled up, and I couldn't get a permit."

Michelle says, "Good."

Following lunch and resting, they are leaving the campground when Nichole says, "Dad?"

Daniel replies, "Go ahead and go back to the restroom. Michelle, please go with her. We will wait here."

Beginning their trek back up to the rim, Daniel remembers hiking with Emily down to Phantom Ranch.

Daniel, walking beside Emily as a party who are riding mules passes them, says, "Maybe we should have taken that way down. What do you say we steal a couple of those mules? You distract them."

Emily says, "Are you kidding me? No thanks. Did you see the way those people were walking earlier? I would much rather be worn down from hiking than from riding a freaking mule."

"Yeah, you're right. They were walking pretty funny."

She says, "I cannot wait to get to Phantom Ranch. I want to lie down on a bed and stretch out."

Daniel says, "Me too, but we still have a ways to go. I need to pee really bad."

"It is only a little farther to the Bright Angel Campground. Can you hold it until then?"

"No, I really need to go."

"Well, step over there. I will watch out for you and let you know if someone comes up."

Daniel says, "Thanks." He finds a spot and calls out to Emily. "Hey, Em, I found a really big snake over here!"

Emily responds, "That must be the cheesiest line you

have ever given me. Don't forget: I have seen you naked." As she walks over closer to where Daniel is, she sees a large rattlesnake on the ground next to a bush a foot away from him. "Oh, shit!"

"Yeah, I would rather not. Taking a piss is bad enough. What should I do?"

Emily tells him, "Just don't move."

"I really wasn't planning to. I still need to pee."

"You mean you haven't gone yet?"

Daniel yells out, "No!" Then, after startling the snake, he says more softly, "No. I didn't think peeing on a snake was a good idea."

Emily says, "Well, keep your voice down. You don't want to startle it any more than it already is."

"I am standing here with my junk out. What if someone comes by?"

Emily tells him, "Try putting it away slowly, without it going off."

"It's not a gun. Okay I will try." Daniel slowly zips up his shorts.

"Now, step back..." Before Emily can finish, Daniel jumps back as the snake strikes, just barely missing his ankle. Laughing, she says, "I was going to say slowly, but that will work, too."

Daniel, relieved, starts walking around and decides to have a seat. Sitting down, he jumps up, screaming. Emily, turning in his direction, starts laughing so hard she begins to cry. Daniel turns back to see he had sat on a large barrel cactus. Emily says, "Wow! I bet that hurts. What were you thinking?"

"I thought it was a boulder."

She replies, "Since when did rocks become coated with

thorns?" When Emily finally catches her breath from laughing, she spends the next hour picking stickers out of Daniel.

After he and the kids pass the three-mile Rest House, the trail becomes much steeper. Continuing to climb, Daniel's thoughts are brought back to the present when Michelle says, "Is this ever going to end? It just goes on forever and forever. I don't think we'll ever get back to the top."

Daniel tells her, "Oh yeah, I forgot to tell you... This section is called Jacob's Ladder. The switchbacks seem like they go on forever."

Nichole, out of breath, asks, "Dad, what are switchbacks?"

Daniel answers, "Switchbacks are these zigzags in the trail that makes it easier to go up and down steep areas."

Nichole says, "It doesn't feel easier."

Daniel tells them, "Just be glad the trail is wide and these switchbacks give us this amazing view."

On the path, a couple is heading down their way when Nichole calls out to them, "Hey! Uphill hikers have the right of way."

Daniel taps her on the shoulder, shaking his head no as she looks up at him and telling her, "Nichole, be nice. You need to be polite when talking to people."

Nichole says, "Sorry, Dad."

Niles begins pulling on Daniel's pant leg. "What is it buddy?" Niles stretches his arms out. "You want me to carry you on my shoulders?" Niles nods yes. Daniel picks him up, carrying him the rest of the way.

Following a day of hiking, they grab some supplies and head back to the campground for a hot-dog-and-s'mores night on the campfire.

Once back at the campground, they see a tall woman with gray hair. She appears to be in her late forties, is camped beside them, and is taking photographs. She comes over and introduces herself with a British accent as they are all working together to build their campfire.

"Hello, you folks. My name is Sally Reiner. I am a travel writer and photographer doing a story on the Grand Canyon."

Daniel says, "Nice to meet you, Sally. My name is Daniel, and this is my oldest daughter Michelle."

Sally says, "Hello, Michelle."

Michelle replies. "Hi."

"My youngest daughter, Nichole..."

"Hello, Nichole."

Nichole says, "Hello. You talk funny."

"Nichole!" Daniel says, "Sorry. She has a way with words."

Sally says, "No worries," She looks at Nichole. "That is because I am originally from England. Where I am from, they say you talk funny, too."

"This is my son Niles."

Loudly, she says to him, with his headphones on, "Nice to meet you, Niles. I like your name." Niles looks at her and smiles.

"And this is my nephew Nathan."

"Hello, Nathan."

Softly, Nathan responds, "Hey."

Daniel says, "We are just in the process of building a fire, and then we are going to roast hot dogs and s'mores. Would you like to join us?"

Michelle says, "You mean burn. Every time you roast hot dogs, you burn them."

Sally replies, "Oh, I would hate to impose."

Daniel says, "You would not be imposing at all. We have more than enough food."

Sally responds, "Yeah, sure. Why not? If you don't mind..."

Daniel tells her, "No, not at all. So, what type of travel photography do you do?"

She replies, "I do mostly freelance work for various travel journals. Sometimes, I am contracted for certain publications, like road atlases, but mainly freelance."

Daniel says, "That sounds like a really nice job."

"It pays the bills, and I get to see the world at the same time. It is better than the alternative of sitting in a war zone in the Middle East."

"I definitely say I have to agree with you there. So, you are from England?"

Sally replies, "Yes, but I am an American citizen now. I've been here in the States for a little over ten years, but I try and visit back home once or twice a year."

Daniel smiles, "On someone else's dime."

Laughing Sally says, "Yes, Daniel, sometimes on someone else's dime."

. . .

DANIEL, after roasting the hot dogs and s'mores, is sitting by the fire with Sally, while Nathan, Niles, and the girls are roaming the campground, walking off their dinner.

Sally says, "If you don't mind me asking, why does your little boy... Niles is it?" Daniel nods. "Why does Niles not seem to say much, or anything actually? Is he just really shy? And his headphones are not plugged into anything."

"You are not the first and I am sure will not be the last to ask that."

She says, "I hope I am not out of line by asking. I suppose it is the observations I am trained to make as a journalist that makes me so inquisitive."

"No, not at all. We lost their mother last year."

Sally replies somberly, "I am so sorry. If it is too difficult, you do not have to say any more."

"No, it is fine. I say that it is fine. How everything is going, though, is probably everything but fine. See, Niles... When my wife Emily was alive, you could not make him stop talking - just constantly, day and night. He even used to talk in his sleep. Niles has always been a very inquisitive child, asking lots of questions all the time. Then, when their mom died, he immediately just stopped talking."

Sally replies, "I am so sorry."

"Thank you. The clinical psychologist diagnosed him with Selective Progressive Mutism: when someone who is able to speak just suddenly stops. Even if staying silent means they may be punished or shamed, they still will not speak. I hoped getting him therapy would be enough to help him unlearn, so to speak, his condition. He is pretty much a textbook case. If you can get him to smile or stare at you, that is a good day. We have been working with a cognitive behavioral therapist to try and redirect his emotions into positive feelings. Nothing seems to be working, though. Every doctor we speak to says the same thing. They tell us they feel a change in environment might be good for him - that this trip might be good for him."

Sally asks, "Is this vacation you are on... Is it for him to get away?"

"No. This is a trip that my wife planned for us to take. Before she passed, she gave me specific directions on what to do, when to go, what to drive, and even the route. As sharp as she was, I cannot imagine she would have had the foresight of knowing Niles would possibly need this. I say that, but at the same time, knowing her, I wouldn't be surprised. So, I guess back to your question... He wears the headphones day and night. He even tries to take baths with them on. I suppose they are like a shield for him, to protect him from the outside world. I don't know if you noticed, but he also wears a whistle around his neck to get my attention." Daniel begins laughing. "Sometimes that works a little too well. Back to what I said about him not speaking: Even when there might be consequences, he won't say a word. A few months ago, I dressed him up as Harry Potter. He had on the round black glasses, a tie, a robe, a wand... the whole get up. Then, I get a call from his school. They said he was picked on by the other kids all day because Storybook Day was the following week." Daniel laughs, and Sally joins him. "Looking back, I could tell he knew it by the look in his eyes while dressing him up. He had this 'What the hell are you doing to me?' look." Again, they both laugh. "But, he didn't say a word. He just went off to school. Niles is a really smart kid. He and Emily... They both were, and they were so close. Emily was close to all the kids - even Michelle, who just about drives me crazy sometimes."

Sally says, "You know what they say about teenagers. The reason they grow so fast is for their own survival. They know they will be too big to bury the body." They both laugh.

Daniel replies, "Amen to that. Even with Niles's condition, I have to say Michelle has taken it the hardest. I mean, you do all you can to protect your children, but some things get past you. She would sit with her mother for long hours when Emily was in bed. She would try to cook and clean, and she read for hours about her mother's illness. I had to sit down with her and explain that it is okay to show emotion. It is okay to be angry. It is okay to be sad. It is okay to cry, and it's okay to just be yourself. I told her to see her friends and keep a journal to write down what she is feeling - what we all were feeling. When Emily died, I explained to them there is no right way or wrong way to grieve. We all have to deal with it in our own way, but I know they were always watching me, trying to learn how to do it. Michelle was just entering adolescence. She had butted heads with Emily a few times, and she was regretting those arguments. I carry a lot of regret myself. I was always on the road for work, and I missed so much time with all of them." Daniel pauses. "Let me know if I start boring you with my life."

"No, not at all, Daniel. Go ahead."

He tells her, "Well, backtracking a little, I met their mom in college. Our senior year, we moved into our first apartment. It was near campus, and Emily was so glad to be out of her dorm. We were so glad to be together every possible moment. It was a two-bedroom apartment. We turned the second bedroom into an office for me and an art studio for her. She made such beautiful paintings. They were of the ocean, sunrises and sunsets, and the night sky. I so miss watching Emily work on her paintings." Daniel pauses, lost in his thoughts. "Sorry. I got a little sidetracked."

"No worries."

He continues, "So, living together, college life changed. It was no more about parties, social events, and did I say parties?" They both laugh. "Suddenly, it was about spending every moment I had with her. The night of my graduation, my parents were killed in a plane crash."

Sally responds, "Oh, Daniel. I am so sorry. How awful. Was it a commercial flight?"

"No, it was private. My dad had his pilot's license and owned a small plane. Well, after that, we cancelled our formal wedding and eloped. Following the wedding, I began working immediately. Not being able to keep our hands off each other, it was just a matter of time before Michelle was born. After three years as a stay at home mom, Emily was preparing to start her career as a real-estate agent when nature decided Michelle needed a little sister. I got there just barely in time to see Nichole born. My career was taking off. The pay was amazing for someone fresh out of college, but far too often it took me away from home. Emily hated it. After Niles was born, I was back on a plane within two hours. In reflection, I now realize the time away ended up costing me much more than any amount of money I could have ever made."

"Daniel, you should never feel regret. No one can see what the future may bring."

"I know. We have come a long way over the last year. At first, we all had trouble sleeping. It seems to be getting better, though, with time - not good, just better. I even sent the kids to a bereavement group with other children - just anything to protect them - anything to try help them heal. Gosh, we would go through photo albums and talk about old stories, like the time I put baby powder all over our hardwood floor. We were all playing indoor hockey, wearing hockey jerseys and socks. I ended up falling flat on my back and had to be taken to the emergency room." They laugh. "I am sorry. I have just rambled on this evening. I'm sorry. That was a lot more than you wanted to hear, I'm sure."

Sally says, "No. I am glad you told me."

"I suppose, in summary, it is all the emotional complexities of being a parent."

"From what I have heard, I think it is a little more than that. Daniel, I think you are a really good father, and I bet you were an amazing husband."

"Thank you, Sally. Today, I was wondering when the memories that flash before me whenever I see something that reminds me of her will end."

Sally says, "Hopefully never. I am no psychologist, but I think you should cherish every time that happens. Focus on the good times you two shared - the happy memories and all the happy times you were there for each other."

At that moment, the kids walk back up to the campsite and Michelle says, "Thanks for dinner, Dad. You did a nice job not burning it this time."

Daniel says, "Hey, be nice."

Michelle tries again, "All right. Thank you for not burning dinner."

Laughing, he says, "Okay, that sounded much better, I think. Time to start getting ready for bed. We head out early tomorrow morning."

Sally says, "Yes, it is way past my bedtime, as well. Thank you again for dinner and a nice talk, Daniel. I will see you folks in the morning."

Daniel says, "Goodnight, Sally."

"Goodnight, Daniel, and..." Pointing at each child, she says, "Goodnight, Michelle, Niles, Nichole, and... Nathan."

As everyone is preparing for bed, Daniel hears a scream. He runs over to Michelle, who is standing outside their tent entrance. Beside the zipper is a frog that has suctioned himself to the front of the tent. Daniel says, "Everybody, calm down. It is just a little tree frog."

Michelle says, "What it is, is gross." Daniel, reaching his finger toward it, says, "It's not gross. It's cute." Suddenly, the frog leaps off the tent onto Daniel's nose. He lets out a screeching, high-pitched scream, and the girls join in.

The frog, with a little help from Daniel, flies off his face, and Michelle says, "It is just a cute little tree frog, remember?"

Everyone is laughing at, and with, Daniel. He even got a smile out of Niles. As the family steps into their tent, Daniel says, "Okay, the excitement is over. It's time to get ready for bed."

The following morning, everyone is up early, as they plan to catch breakfast on their way out of the park. Walking from the bus, Daniel is wearing his Counting Crows concert shirt and jeans, when he walks past Michelle. She says politely, "Nice shirt, Dad."

Daniel thinks to himself that hell must have just frozen over, since he actually received a compliment from his teenage daughter about his wardrobe. In return, he decides to show his awareness of her trying, perhaps for the first time in a very long time, to attempt to have a conversation with him longer than a sentence. He says to her, "Are you not going to wear any makeup today?"

Michelle begins crying, running back into the tent. "What did I say wrong?"

Nichole, who is watching it all says, "Dad, she already has it on."

Daniel responds, "Great."

Nichole asks, "Dad?"

"Daughter?"

"Why do women have to wear makeup and men don't?"

Daniel replies, "Women don't need to, but some think it makes them prettier when they do."

"Dad, maybe you should try wearing makeup."

"Thanks Nichole. Thanks a lot."

She says, smiling, "You're welcome."

ONCE THE BUS is all packed up, Sally walks up to Daniel. "Would you mind if I get a photo of all of you in front of the bus?"

"No, not at all. I was about to ask you if you would. Will you get one with my phone, as well?"

Sally replies, "Certainly."

Daniel says, "Hey, everybody, gather around for a picture."

They all line up beside the bus, Daniel and Nathan in the back with the girls and Niles in the front. Before Sally can take the photo, Nichole calls out, "Wait! What about mom?" She goes into the bus and comes out with her jar wrapped in her arms. Once everyone is ready, Sally takes the photos.

While saying goodbye, Sally asks Daniel, "Daniel,

would you mind if I did a write up about you and your family?"

Daniel responds, "No, not at all."

She says, "Great, I will email you a release and probably have a lot more questions to ask."

"No problem. We will be back home in about three weeks, and I can respond then."

"Thank you. Everyone, enjoy your trip. It was nice meeting you all." Daniel and Sally exchange email addresses before heading back out on the open road.

SEDONA

Pulling into Sedona, Daniel says to Michelle, "Michelle! Oh my god! You are still alive."

She asks, "What... What do you mean?"

Laughing, Daniel tells her, "You survived almost two days without the internet." She rolls her eyes as she puts her earbuds in. "Okay gang, who is hungry?"

Michelle and Nichole scream out, "Me!" Niles raises his hand, and Nathan stays silent, staring out the window and lost in his thoughts.

Daniel says, "This, my children, is Sedona. People say, 'God created the Grand Canyon, but he lives in Sedona.'"

Nichole asks, "God lives here? I thought he was in heaven somewhere."

Daniel tells her, "What they mean is Sedona is like heaven. It's a magical place. Near some of the rock formations here, they have what are called energy vortexes."

Nichole asks, "What do you mean energy more taxes?"

Michelle says, "Vortexes, you moron."

Nichole yells, "Shut up!"

Then, Michelle responds, "No, you shut up!"

Nichole again says, "No, you shut up!"

Daniel tells them, "Both of you shut up! Nichole, vortexes are specific locations where natural electromagnetic energies from the earth intersect. Not everyone, but some people can actually feel it at some or all of the locations here. I only felt it at one of them on all my trips here."

Nichole asks, "Dad, what does it feel like?"

He says, "I felt a tingling on my arm and a tickling on the back of my neck. Hey! Look to your left. See that ridge off in the distance? That is called Snoopy Rock. It looks like Snoopy on top of his dog house."

Nichole screams, "I see it!"

Michelle says, "No, I'm not seeing it."

Daniel replies pointing, "Look right over there."

Michelle says, "Oh, okay. I see it. Cool."

Daniel asks Niles, "Niles, did you guys see it? Nathan?"

Nichole answers, "Niles nods his head yes."

Nathan says, "Yeah, I saw it. I'm hungry."

Daniel says, "Good, because we are going to stop at my favorite place to eat here: The Red Planet Diner. It's like a 50s diner meets the X-Files."

Nichole says, "Cool! What do they have?"

He replies, "They have burgers, reubens, chili cheeseburgers, milkshakes, and meatloaf that they call moonloaf."

Nichole says, "Moonloaf? That's funny."

He tells them, "Here we are."

Michelle says, "Hey look, there is a flying saucer out front."

Nichole says, "Cool!"

They enter the restaurant and are immediately struck by the decor. There are alien dolls hanging from the ceiling, which is painted with stars. In the center of the ceiling, the bottom of a flying saucer is sticking out, and inside the jukebox are alien dolls playing guitars.

When they take a seat at their table, they cannot help but notice a woman telling a man taking notes about her most recent alien abduction, due primarily to the volume of her voice. They all look at one another, trying not to laugh. From what they could tell, the man was doing research on alien abductions, and the woman was claiming to have had over seventy-five of these encounters.

Nichole says, "Dad?"

"Yes, Daughter?"

"I will never get taken by aliens."

Michelle says, "That is because when you start talking they would bring you back."

Nichole says, "Shut up!"

Daniel says, "Hey, you two! Why Nichole? Why would the aliens not abduct you?"

Nichole says, "The aliens would not take me because I know not to talk to strangers. If an alien offered me some candy to ride in his UFO, I would tell him, 'No,' and start screaming, 'Alien stranger danger!' That's why."

Michelle laughs and says, "Oh Lord."

Following their meal, Daniel takes them around to see some of the sights. First, they visit the Airport Mesa. Then they go to the Chapel of the Holy Cross. Next, they drive to the Courthouse Butte, which Nichole gets a kick out of calling Courthouse Butt, and they end with Bell Rock.

At Bell Rock, they walk up the trail, and Daniel shows them the location where he feels the energy vortex.

He says, "You guys, I can feel it start right here." Then, walking farther up, he says, "And it ends right here."

The kids walk back and forth, but, just like at the other sites, none of them feels anything.

Michelle says, "Dad, I think you are making this stuff up."

Daniel tells them, "It doesn't work with everyone." He can see the frustration of not being able to feel the vortex on Nichole's face, so he points up toward the large hill and says, “Nichole, that is Bell Rock. If you put your ear to the ground, you can hear it ringing.”

Nichole lays down and places her ear to the ground. Laughing, Michelle walks up and asks Daniel, “What is she doing?”

He says, “She is trying to hear the bell ring.”

Michelle says, “Dad, you are a dork.”

Suddenly, Nichole says, “I hear it! I hear it!”

Daniel smiles and says, “Good job.”

As everyone starts walking back to the bus, Michelle lingers while leaning over slightly toward the ground to see if she can hear a ringing. Daniel just laughs to himself. As Michelle catches up with him, he tells her, “If you say gullible really slowly, it sounds like oranges.”

She begins to say it and then tells him in disgust, “Shut up.” Frustrated, she walks to the bus.

Driving around Sedona, Daniel spots a Wendy’s. Immediately, he is taken back to the first date with their mother many years ago. He is also reminded of their first wedding anniversary.

That evening, Emily comes home from work to find a trail of rose petals leading to the bedroom. Her black dress is laid out on the bed with a note from Daniel telling her he will be home to pick her up at seven o'clock and to be ready. Just as it says her, he makes it home at seven, and, even though he has his key, he still rings the doorbell. Emily answers the door in her dress.

Daniel, dressed in a suit, tells her, "You are so beautiful." Reaching for her hand, he escorts her to his bus.

Emily asks, "So where are we going this evening?"

Daniel responds, "Remember that steak dinner I promised you for our first date?"

"Yes, I believe I do."

During their drive, they complement each other on their attire. Emily says, "So, I finally get to see this elegant restaurant you talked about years ago."

"Kind of." Daniel says, as he pulls into a Wendy's parking lot, and he parks by the door.

Emily says, "Wendy's again?" Daniel can sense the disappointment in her voice, even though she tries to hide it. "You know, you cannot park here."

Just then, wearing a black tux and white gloves, Daniels's fraternity brother Jason opens Emily's door. In a matching tux and gloves, another brother of his, Kennedy, opens Daniel's door. Daniel hands Kennedy his keys so he can park his bus. Daniel walks over to Emily, taking her arm, as Jason opens the doors for them. Emily is not saying a word, only smiling, giggling, and shaking her head.

Jason escorts them to the front corner of the restaurant

while people eating inside are staring at them walking through. He escorts the couple to the corner that has been blocked off by a black curtain hanging from the ceiling with fishing line. Jason pulls the curtain aside, allowing them to enter. Waiting inside is a table with a white dinner cloth, candles, fine silverware, and crystal wine glasses.

Emily asks, "What did you do this time?"

Smiling, Daniel replies, "The owner is a Kappa Sigma alumni."

Jason says, after pulling Emily's chair out for her to sit in, "Your server will be with you in a moment."

Then, Kennedy walks in carrying two plates with a giant steak and French fries on each one. He places them in front of the couple. Daniel says, "Thank you, my good sir." Jason then enters with a bottle of wine, while Kennedy exits. Jason presents them with the cork before he pours their glasses. Daniel responds, "Very nice."

Jason exits, and Kennedy enters, carrying a large squeeze-bottle of mayonnaise and holds it out, displaying it for their approval like a bottle of wine. Daniel says, "Very good." Kennedy then places it on the table. That is the moment Emily loses it. She begins laughing and crying at the same time.

Emily says, "I love you so much, Daniel."

Daniel stands and walks over to kiss her on the cheek. "I love you, too, Em. Happy anniversary, my beautiful bride."

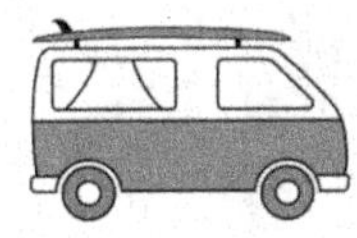

Daniel is brought back to reality by the girls arguing in the back seat.

Nichole says, sticking her tongue out at Michelle, "Michelle is texting her boyfriend back home."

Michelle says, "No, I'm not! Mind your own business!"

Nichole keeps sticking her tongue out, saying, "Michelle has a boyfriend. Michelle has a boyfriend."

Michelle replies, "No, I don't! Stop it!"

Daniel says, "Nichole be quiet. Stop picking on your sister."

Nichole replies, "I am not picking on her."

Michelle says, "Yes, you are!"

Daniel tells them, "Both of you be quiet. Do you know that every time you act bad, your parents get more grey hairs?"

Nichole replies, "Mommy must have been really bad because Grandma and Poppy have so many grey hairs."

Laughing, Daniel says, "You're probably right."

Farther down the road, as it is getting late, Daniel tells them, "Okay, guys, I was hoping to make it to Albuquerque tonight, but I'm getting too tired, and Nathan does not have a driver's license. I am going to pull into the next hotel we see." When he finishes his statement, he looks into the rearview mirror, finding everyone sound asleep. "Okay, so none of you heard me anyway." He exits the interstate and pulls into a tiny motel. "Well, they have one sign that says vacancy, and another, simply Motel. Looks like it should be called The Last Option Motel. Okay, everybody up! Wake up! You all stay here. I am going to check in and will be right back."

Michelle mumbles, "Where are we?"

Daniel gets out and is opening the door to the motel office, when Nichole steps in front of him, walking through the door, saying, "Thank you."

He says, "I thought I told you to wait in the bus."

Smiling, Nichole responds, "Well, I thought you might need some help."

AFTER CHECKING IN, Daniel gets the keys, and they all pile into their rooms.

Michelle says, "This place is a dump."

"Well, as tired as I am, it was the only option this late at night, so it will have to do. Okay, we have both rooms, two beds in each room. Michelle, you and your sister take this room."

Nichole calls out, "I call dibs on this bed!"

Michelle tells her, "They are both the same. It doesn't matter."

Daniel says, "Girls, keep this door between the rooms open at all times. Nathan and I will take this other room." Looking down at Niles, he says, "You, my little man, can sleep in bed with me."

Daniel steps over to the girls' room to spray the monster spray. He finds the girls arguing about the beds.

He says, "Michelle, you just said both beds are the same. Why does it matter?"

Nichole says, "She only wants this bed because I wanted it first."

Daniel tells them, "Okay, Michelle, you are in this bed. Nichole, you take that one. Problem solved. Nichole, make sure to brush your teeth, or they will all fall out." Again looking down at Niles, he says, "You too, Little Man."

Nichole says, "I want them to fall out so the tooth fairy

will bring me more money. Then, I'll be rich!"

Niles starts nodding his head yes vigorously, as if to say, "Me too."

Daniel replies, "That is not how it works."

Nichole says, "It should be."

Michelle chimes in, "There is no such thing as the tooth fairy, anyway. Fairies don't exist."

Nichole says, "Yes they do! Atticus is a fairy, and he is real!"

Michelle says, "Oh, brother." Then Niles peaks into their room with his toothbrush in his mouth. "No, Niles, I was not talking about you. 'Oh brother' is just a figure of speech." Then, he shrugs his shoulders, and he returns to brushing his teeth.

AFTER EVERYONE IS in bed and the lights are out, Nichole leaves her room. She climbs into bed with Daniel and Niles, holding her fairy figurine.

Daniel asks, "What's up, Short Stuff?"

Nichole says, "I had a dream Mommy came back to us, but then I woke, and she wasn't there."

Comforting her, he says, "It is okay, Sweetheart. Daddy has the same dream all the time. It will get easier. I promise."

She asks, "What if something happens to you, too?"

Daniel replies, "Daddy isn't going anywhere. I will always be here for you and your brother and your sister."

"You promise?"

He says, "I promise."

"You pinky promise?"

Reaching out his pinky for hers, Daniel says, "I pinky promise."

THE BEST LAID PLANS OF MICE AND MEN

When Daniel wakes up the next morning, he finds Nichole up, playing with a tiny mouse she found in the bathroom. He says, "Nichole! Get away from that thing!"

She replies, "But, Daddy, he is a cute little mouse. He lets me pet him. See?"

As he chases it away under the dresser, Daniel says, "Nichole, leave it alone now."

Nichole responds, "But, Daddy, he was my friend."

Daniel tells her, "Time for us to get up and get moving so you can make other friends - friends that talk and walk on two legs. Come on, everybody! Up and at 'em!"

They get the bus loaded and again hit the road. On the way out of the little town they stayed in, Daniel sees a man out for a morning jog alongside the road. He is taken back to his morning jogs with Emily and the day everything began changing in their lives.

Daniel and Emily go out one morning for one of their daily runs before work. Emily has always been an excellent sprinter and long-distance runner, back to her high school days. Today, unlike the other mornings, Emily falls back. Daniel looks to his side and does not see her. Looking back, he catches a glimpse of Emily doubled over, out of breath, and exhausted. Daniel runs back to check on her, asking, "You okay?"

Emily replies, "Yes. I am just a little tired today. I must have worked out too hard yesterday at the gym."

The two of them walk back to their home, and Emily jumps in the shower first. While rinsing off, Emily discovers a large lump in her right breast. It had been a while since she took the time to do a breast self-exam, so she immediately wonders how long it has been there. Once out of the shower, she puts on her makeup and coaches the kids, who are preparing their lunches for school.

Together, they drop off the kids at school. Then, she drives Daniel to the airport for an eleven-day business trip to Minneapolis. After kissing him goodbye and leaving the airport, she stops by her office to pick up some new listings for the houses she is going to show that day. On the way to the office, she calls her doctor and makes an appointment for the following day. Daniel has an important presentation to give, and she does not want to worry him about her discovery that morning.

THE NEXT DAY at her OB/GYN's office, Emily sits in the waiting room, trying to keep her mind off why she is there. Once called back, Dr. Rene Sutherland examines Emily's breasts.

Dr. Sutherland tells her, "Emily, I am a little concerned with the size and the shape. I am going to order an MRI for tomorrow."

Emily asks, "An MRI? Why not a mammogram?"

The doctor says, "As young as you are... Younger women tend to have denser breast tissue, so an MRI will give us a better picture."

Emily asks, "So, should I be concerned?"

"It may be nothing. I would not worry."

Emily responds, "But it maybe something?"

The doctor replies, "Let's just wait for the results. Okay?"

"Okay."

LITTLE DID Emily know at the time, her lump was a textbook large, irregularly shaped, solid mass, that would change all of their lives forever.

Emily, on her evening call with Daniel, still makes no mention of the events of her day.

. . .

THE NEXT MORNING, she goes in for her tests. Following the tests, she still finds no comfort in Dr. Sutherland's words from the day before, and her concern continues to grow.

THE FOLLOWING DAY, Emily gets a phone call from Dr. Sutherland's nurse. She answers, "Hello, this is Emily."

"Yes, this is Monica from Dr. Sutherland's office."

Emily says, "Oh, hello. Did the doctor get the results back?"

"Yes, she did. There were some abnormalities, so Dr. Sutherland is requesting a biopsy from Dr. Mara Patel."

Emily asks, "A biopsy?"

"Yes, Dr. Patel is an oncologist."

Surprised, Emily responds, "An oncologist?"

"Yes, I can give you her office number. Do you have something to write with?"

Frustrated, Emily snaps back, "Of course I don't. I am driving down the damn street."

"I'm sorry, ma'am, but I can text it to you. Would you like me to text it?"

Much calmer, Emily replies, "Yes. Thank you."

"I will have it to you in just a moment. Goodbye."

Emily says, "Goodbye." She screams, while punching the steering wheel. "Fuck!" Fuck! Fuck! Fuck... Fuck!"

THAT AFTERNOON, Emily contacts Dr. Patel's office for an appointment. At her appointment the following day with Dr. Patel, the doctor explains the results and recommendations to Emily.

Dr. Patel asks, "Mrs. White, have any of your family

members ever had lumps or been diagnosed with breast cancer?"

Emily replies, "Yes, my grandmother and my aunt. Both had lumps, but neither had cancer."

"That's good, then. That gives us more hope that yours will be the same."

"Fingers crossed."

Dr. Patel has Emily take off her shirt and examines her breasts. She presses under Emily's right arm, asking, "Does that hurt?"

Emily replies, "Just a little."

Dr. Patel says, "Okay, you can put your top back on. I am somewhat concerned about the size. On the MRI, it appears to be a little over 5 centimeters. With that size, I would feel better doing a surgical biopsy instead of a needle biopsy. With a needle biopsy, we draw a sample out with a needle. With yours, I would like to have a larger sample to test."

Emily asks, "Will the surgical biopsy leave a scar?"

The doctor replies, "We will go in with a curved incision at the base of your areola, so the appearance of scarring is kept to a minimum. You will, however, have some soreness and swelling. Again, due to the size, I would shy away from an excisional biopsy, in which we remove the entire lump. Removing that much tissue tends to leave one breast smaller than the other. I would like to do an incisional biopsy and only take just the amount of tissue we need to test. The only drawback is, if we do find something abnormal, we have to go back in again and then remove it all. During the biopsy, we will place a tiny titanium clip about the size of a sesame seed to mark the area where the tissue was removed. This will give us a marker, a reference point, to look for any changes in any future tests we might possibly have to do. The biopsy is an outpatient procedure, so you will not have to stay overnight. So how does that sound to you?"

"Fine, I guess. Just... My husband is out of town on business, so I will need to check with my sister in law to see if she can watch my children."

The doctor asks, "How many children do you have, Mrs. White?"

Emily replies, "I have three: two daughters... one just turned twelve, and the other is seven going on eight... and a little boy, who just turned four."

"Oh, what cute ages. Just wait until they are teenagers - not so cute anymore, then."

Emily says, "Yeah, I can already tell I am going to have my hands full with the oldest one. How long will I have to wait for the results?"

"We should have some results in two or three days following the biopsy. Any more questions?"

Emily replies, "No, I think that is it."

Dr. Patel says, "Just let them know up front what day is good for you. Thank you, Mrs. White."

"Thank you, doctor."

Emily is able to get scheduled for the biopsy two days out. That evening, she calls Beverly, who agrees to watch the children. She also gets Beverly's word that she will not mention it to Daniel. Emily contacts her friend Susan and arranges for her to drive her there and take her home following the procedure.

. . .

The biopsy is performed, and the waiting begins. Over the next two days, she experiences fear, anxiety, and disbelief. The hardest part of it all is keeping all these emotions to herself.

The waiting has passed, and, as Emily is driving down Melrose Avenue in her Armada, she receives a call from Dr. Patel.

She answers, "Hello."

"Mrs. White?"

Emily replies, "Yes."

"This is Dr. Patel. How are you?"

"I don't know, doctor. You tell me."

Dr. Patel says, "Yes, that is what I was calling about. I received your results, and the tissue samples did show to be malignant." Emily begins crying. "I would like to see you in my office at nine o'clock in the morning to talk about some treatments. Can you be here for this? Hello... Mrs. White?"

Trying to collect herself, Emily replies, "Yes, I will be there."

"Thank you, Mrs. White. I will see you in the morning. Goodbye."

Emily says, "Goodbye." She then screams to the top of her lungs. "Fuck!" She breaks down in tears, and she calls Daniel, getting his voicemail. At this point, Emily is crying so hard she can hardly see the road.

Daniel immediately calls her back. He asks, "Em, what's wrong?"

Emily replies, "Oh Daniel, please come home." She is having difficulty formulating words. "Daniel, I have cancer."

He pauses and responds, "What? Where?"

"It is in my right breast. Oh, Daniel, please come home."

He says, "I am on my way. I will take the next flight.

"Daniel, I need you."

Trying to reassure her, he tells her, "I will be there as fast as I can Em. I will call you with the flight information. I love you, Em."

"I love you, too, Daniel." She replies, and she hangs up.

Looking up, she finds herself stopped in the middle of Highland Avenue facing the wrong way. The oncoming traffic is blaring their horns as they pass. A police officer pulls up in front of her and stops traffic, allowing her get turned around, and she drives straight home.

Daniel arrives home that night. Emily tells him everything that has occurred over the last several days.

Daniel asks, "Em, why did you not tell me?"

Emily answers, crying, "You had your presentation to do. You have been preparing for it for weeks."

"Dammit, Em. I would have rescheduled it."

She says, "I knew if I told you, you would have worried and been unable to focus."

"No, because I wouldn't have gone in the first place."

"Daniel, I'm scared."

Daniel puts his arms around her, their foreheads pressed together. He tells her, "Em, it is going to be okay. We will get through this."

The next day, they meet with Dr. Patel.

Emily introduces Daniel to Dr. Patel. The doctor says, "Pleasure to meet you, Mr. White."

Daniel shakes her hand, and replies, "I wish I could say the same, doc."

"I understand. I know the two of you have many questions. Let me start with what I know, and perhaps some of your questions might get answered. Okay?"

While sitting in a chair next to Daniel and holding his hand, Emily responds, "Yes."

Dr. Patel says, "First off, the lump was a little larger than expected." Emily grips Daniel's hand tighter. "Larger does not always mean fast growing, like a small lump does not mean slow growing. The lump in your right breast turned out to be about 7 centimeters. The tissue sample we took came back ER negative, PR negative, and HER2 positive. Let me explain what this means. First off ER stands for Estrogen Receptors, and PR stands for Progesterone Receptors. With an ER and a PR negative result it tells us that the cancer cells do not have either hormone. Not containing either hormone means any form of hormonal therapy would be ineffective; however, there are other treatments we will discuss. First, let us look at the HER2 positive result. HER2 is the Human Epidermal growth factor Receptor 2. HER2 controls protein on the cells' surface to help them grow. HER2 positive tells us it is not functioning properly. The positive means your cells are making too many copies of themselves. We call this gene amplification, which results in too much protein being made. This, we call protein overexpression. Your cancer cells are growing, copying themselves at a fast rate."

A tear starts running down Emily's cheek, and her grip on Daniel's hand grows even tighter. She asks, "So, what happens now?"

Dr. Patel replies, "Our next step should be a lumpectomy, in which we remove the cancer tissue and a small amount of healthy tissue around it, just to be safe."

Emily says aloud to herself, "And I was worried about a little scar."

Dr. Patel says, "Yes, well, with this size of tumor, once the tissue is removed, there will be a substantial decrease in your breast size."

Emily takes a deep breath in.

"I also feel we should do a sentinel lymph node biopsy. We would first inject a blue dye in the area of the cancer. The dye will travel to the sentinel lymph nodes. Then, I will be able to locate them. With a small incision, I will remove one to perhaps as many as three lymph nodes from under the right arm, the nodes where the breast drains. This will let us see if the cancer has spread to the lymph nodes. It will help me determine how invasive the cancer might be."

Emily asks, "What happens then?"

"If no cancer shows in the sentinel lymph nodes, then we can be free of most worries."

"What if it does show?"

The Dr. replies, "If it does show, we could possibly do an axillary lymph node dissection, to remove more lymph nodes. All that is a big if. First, let us do the lumpectomy and the sentinel biopsy, and we will go from there." Placing her hand on Emily's shoulder, she tells her, "Do not worry about the unknown. Do not worry about what has not happened. In life, we seem too often to borrow troubles. Okay?"

Nodding her head, Emily says, "Okay."

Before leaving the room, Dr. Patel says, "All right. It was nice meeting you, Mr. White. Emily we will get you scheduled."

Daniel says, "Thank you."

. . .

Two days later, following the lumpectomy and the sentinel biopsy, Emily and Daniel find themselves back in Dr. Patel's office to learn the results.

Entering the exam room, Dr. Patel says, "Thank you both for coming in today. I have the results for you. The sentinel lymph node biopsy does show the cancer has spread."

Emily immediately cries out, "No..." Bursting into tears, she buries her face into Daniel's chest.

Daniel asks, "So, now what?"

Emily, still crying, says, "I will have to have a mastectomy!"

Dr. Patel responds, "That is not necessarily the case, Mrs. White. Before we do anything else, I have a few more tests I would like to have run today, if you have the time. We will need at least five hours for testing. Do you have the time today?"

Daniel answers for her, "Yes, we do."

"Excellent. I would like to order an MRI, a PET scan, a bone scan, and a CT scan. Then I want to see you back here tomorrow morning at this same time. Okay?"

Emily replies, "Okay. Why a bone scan?"

"With secondary breast cancer, the bones tend to be a highly likely site for spreading. It does this through the blood and the lymphatic tissue."

Daniel asks, "What does it entail?"

"We inject radioactive materials into a vein. The material circulates to different sites in the body. All the areas where the material collects indicate locations where cells and tissues are repairing themselves. The nuclear images highlight those areas for us. Any more questions?"

Emily answers, "No, I think that is all for now."

"Great, I will have a nurse get those tests scheduled. You can sit in the waiting room, and someone from radiology will come get you. Also, here is some reading material, along with a few websites to better help you to understand what all is occurring. Thank you both again for coming in." Patting Emily's back, Dr. Patel reassures her, "It will be all right, dear."

Daniel says, "Thank you."

Dr. Patel tells them, "All right. Take care." A nurse then escorts them back to the waiting room.

EMILY COMPLETES ALL the tests that Dr. Patel ordered. They go home and spend another agonizing night continuing their search for more information online and reading through the material the doctor gave them.

MORNING ARRIVES, and neither of them has slept. Upon arriving at Dr. Patel's office, they are escorted to her personal office today instead of an exam room. This change only adds more fear into Emily's heart. Dr. Patel tells them, "Please have a seat." They sit in the two leather chairs that face the front of her desk.

Dr. Patel says, "Thank you both again for coming in." Daniel and Emily have a tight grip on each other's hands. "I have all the information I need now to assess the situation further. Mrs. White... May I call you Emily?"

With her voice shaking, Emily replies, "Yes."

"Emily, as I shared with you earlier, your original biopsy showed you were ER/PR negative and HER2 positive. Also, we discussed your lymph node issues. Since the cancer had spread to your lymph nodes, I wanted to get a closer look at the rest of your body. I am sure by now you have researched all these results further and have a better understanding of where we are. Emily, I must tell you..." Emily and Daniel have a grip so tight on each other that their hands are turning white from lack of circulation. "Your cancer has spread."

Again, Emily breaks down in tears, and Daniel's head lowers, facing the floor, as he leans toward Emily.

Crying, Emily asks, "Where? Where has it spread?"

"Emily..." Dr. Patel makes eye contact with Daniel, nodding slightly. By her glance and her gesture, Daniel can tell she is about to give Emily terrible news, so he prepares to help calm her. "The PET scan and the CT scan show your cancer has spread to your lungs and liver." The volume of Emily's sobbing increases. "The bone scan shows the cancer has spread to your bones. It is currently in your ribs, pelvis, and skull. Your MRI, along with your other scans, shows cancer has spread to your spine and into your brain."

Emily cries out, "Oh my god! Why? Oh, Daniel."

Dr. Patel tells her, "I am so sorry, Emily."

Daniel tries comforting her. "Em, it is going to be okay. You are going to fight this. And you are going to defeat it."

"Oh, Daniel... our babies. I want to see them grow up."

"Emily, you have stage IV cancer."

Angrily, Emily responds, "What the fuck, doctor? What the hell happened to one, two, and three? I exercise. I eat healthy. It cannot be in my brain. I can fucking quote Chaucer. This cannot be happening. This is not the way I planned it. This is not the plan. This is not the way it is supposed to be."

Dr. Patel says, "Please, Emily... Please just take some deep breaths. Due to the spread, it is inoperable, but there are many treatments we can pursue. Like your husband says, you can fight this, but you must focus and stay focused. I will not give up, and I will not let you give up either."

Daniel asks, while holding Emily, "What's next, doctor?"

Dr. Patel says, "First thing's first. Emily, are you listening to me? Emily?"

Through her tears, collecting herself, Emily answers, "Yes."

Dr. Patel tells her, "We are going to fight this together. Do you understand?"

Softly, Emily replies, "Yes."

"I want you to know, I will always be up front and honest with you. At times, you may not want to hear all I have to say, but I will always be honest with you. So, we know your test was ER and PR negative, so we can rule out hormone therapy. Next, we now know you have an extremely aggressive, invasive cancer. With all we know, I do not recommend the axillary lymph node dissection. In cases such as yours, that just does more harm than good. I also do not recommend a mastectomy. In your situation, there is no evidence that it would give you any better chance of survival. It would just put more strain on your body trying to heal. We are going to start with some targeted therapy medication and radiation therapy. Also, I am going to start you with a AC-TH regimen of chemotherapy, which we can tweak if need be. Chemotherapy is not pleasant, but many patients find it is not nearly as awful as television and movies like to depict. The chemo will help to destroy the cancer cells and keep them from copying themselves. We will do thirty cycles of radiation for the next six weeks, as well as chemo, with six cycles, for three weeks. We will then follow with more scans to see where we are at.

You will need some rest following your chemo sessions. You also need to go home now and let all of this sink in. Maybe go to a favorite restaurant or draw a bubble bath to help calm your thoughts. You will be tempted, I know, to do research, but that can begin tomorrow. Right now, just rest. When you wake up tomorrow morning, I want you to strap on your armor, and the battle can begin. Okay... Okay?"

Emily says, "Yes, okay."

"My nurse will contact you to set up schedule times and medications. If you have any questions, please feel free to call my office. And, Emily, just focus. Remember tomorrow the war begins. Thank you both for meeting with me."

Daniel says, "Thank you, doctor."

Daniel recalls how they spent all that night, holding each other closer than they ever had before.

Suddenly, Daniel is pulled away from his thoughts by the feeling of something moving around in his jeans, from his right knee and along his thigh. He begins moving his leg off the gas pedal and starts swerving on the interstate, just as he passes a New Mexico State Police Officer. Daniel yells out, "Nichole! What did you do with that mouse?!"

Nichole replies, "I brought him with us. I did not want to leave him behind." She looks in her purse and cries out, "Dad, he's gone!"

Daniel calls out, "I found him! Nichole!" His swerving

becomes more erratic. Just then, the trooper behind him turns on his flashing lights. Daniel makes it to the right shoulder and stops, totally oblivious to the officer. Moving his leg from the gas to the brake allowed a wide enough gap in his jeans for the tiny mouse to reach his boxers. Daniel lets out another cry, "Nichole!" He bolts from the bus, running around the front and into the shrubs and sand on the side of the road. The trooper, who was exiting his vehicle at the same moment as Daniel, charges after him. Daniel drops his jeans to his ankles, while running and screaming "Nichole!" This gives the officer time to catch up with him.

The trooper continues yelling out, "On the ground! On the ground! On the ground now!" But, all Daniel can process is this mouse and removing it from his boxers.

Suddenly, the officer tackles him from behind, as again Daniel screams, "Nicholeee!"

The officer places handcuffs on Daniel, stands him up, and asks him, "What the hell is wrong with you?"

Nichole runs out of the bus with Niles following her, his headphone cord blowing in the wind. She begins yelling at the officer, "Let go of my daddy!" Niles is blowing his whistle at the officer, loudly and repeatedly.

While all of this is occurring, Michelle, in the back of the bus, sees Nathan take a bag of marijuana out of his pocket and place it under the seat. Looking up, he sees Michelle staring at him and knows she observed what he did. He places his finger over his mouth, saying, "Shhh..."

Back outside, Daniel is trying to explain to the officer what happened while Nichole is still screaming and Niles is still blowing his whistle. The two children are running around them, like Indians circling a wagon train. By the look in the trooper's eyes, Daniel can tell he thinks he has come across a bunch of lunatics who had just escaped from a mental hospital. After several minutes and another officer responding for assistance, Daniel was able to calm down the kids, explain his story, get his hands released from the handcuffs, and finally pull up his pants.

Once it was all settled, the two – and by then a third - troopers who responded enjoyed a very good laugh at the cost of Daniel's dignity.

After being freed to leave and driving off, Daniel was too emotional to scold Nichole, but she knew by his silence she was in big trouble.

Nichole speaks first, saying, while stretching her arms out as wide as she can, "Dad, I am a muchillion kabillion times sorry."

Michelle says to her, "Those aren't even real words."

Nichole defends herself. "Yes, they are!"

Michelle tells her, "No, they aren't. You just made them up."

Nichole replies, "All words were made up at some time. If not, there wouldn't be any words at all." Niles shakes his head in agreement.

Daniel says, "Nichole, next time I tell you to do something, you do it."

Nichole responds, "I was just worried for him. I was afraid he would get caught in a mousetrap and die."

Michelle tells her, "Now, he will die by getting eaten by a snake in the desert."

Nichole says, "Shut up, no he won't! Will he dad?"

Daniel, ignoring them, speaks aloud, "I have never been handcuffed before in my entire life."

Nichole tells him, "Dad, when bad things happen, it

isn't because they are bad. They are only bad because that is the way you see it." Daniel does not respond. "When you are mad at me, I feel like the center piece of cake - the one that's not an edge piece, the one without any icing on the side of it. No one wants me."

Michelle says, laughing, "Oh lord."

THE MISSION STATEMENT

After a long stretch of driving, Daniel says, while pointing ahead, "Okay, folks, this is Albuquerque. See that mountain over there? It's called the Sandia Mountain Ridge. It's also called Watermelon Mountain."

Nichole calls out, "Watermelon! Why watermelon?"

Daniel says, "At sunset, it takes on a reddish color, and the long ridge at the top... That part looks greenish, like the rind of a watermelon."

Nathan looks up from his phone, "Now, I'm hungry."

Daniel says, "Good, because we are about to have breakfast at one of my favorite restaurants here in Old Town."

Nichole asks, "What is Old Town? I thought we were in Albacurry."

Michelle says, "No moron, Albuquerque."

Nichole responds, "Shut up!"

Daniel says, "Okay, enough you two. Nichole, Old Town is the oldest part of Albuquerque. It was founded in the early 1700s, and they built the town around the plaza. There is a church there which was built in 1793, and there are lots of shops..."

Laughing, Michelle interrupts, "Any shoe stores?"

Daniel, ignoring her, continues, "...and my favorite restaurant here, The Church Street Cafe."

Michelle asks, "No more UFO places, right?"

Daniel answers, "Right. No UFOs. Old Town is almost ten blocks, and the buildings are all old adobe."

Nichole asks, "Adobe? Like Adobe Pinschers?"

Michelle says, "No stupid, adobe not Doberman."

Daniel says, "Adobe is dried mud. The buildings are made of dried mud, not dogs."

Nichole says, "Cool, a mud house... I wish we had a mud house. If we did, I wouldn't have to take my shoes off before coming in because it wouldn't matter."

Michelle says, "Oh, lord. Are you hearing this?"

At the restaurant, they are seated in the courtyard under a trellis covered with grape vines. Following breakfast, they go into several of the shops around the plaza. Leaving one of the shops, an old woman runs after them screaming, "Thief! Thief! Thief!" They are all startled as she runs up to Nathan, shaking her finger at him and saying, "Thief!"

Daniel steps in between her and Nathan, saying, "Everybody, calm down. What seems to be the problem?"

The woman says, "He stole one of our bracelets!"

Everyone's eyes are directed immediately to Nathan, who looks at his wrist. There, he wears his own leather bracelet and sees the one from the shop. "Oh, shit! This isn't what you think. I was trying on several of them to see if they looked good with mine. I got distracted and..."

The woman yells at him again, "Thief!"

Nathan responds, "I'm not a thief. I just forgot to take it off."

Daniel says to her, "It was just a mistake. How much is the bracelet?"

She says, "It's twenty dollars."

Daniel responds, reaching for his wallet, "Twenty... Okay, here is forty for the trouble."

She takes the money and yells out while walking away, "And do not come back into my shop!"

Daniel says to Nathan, "What the hell were you thinking? When are you going to learn?"

Nathan replies, "I didn't mean to..."

Daniel tells him, "Someday, no one will be there to save your ass! You need to grow up!"

Walking away, Nathan says, "It doesn't matter. You won't believe me, anyway."

Daniel calls, "Come back here!"

"Whatever! Nothing I say matters anyway! I will be at your stupid bus! I do not know why you brought me on this stupid trip! I just want to go home!"

THEY STOP by a few more shops, and, upon on leaving, they find Nathan at the bus. Daniel says to him, "I am sorry I blew up at you back there."

Looking down, Nathan says, "Yeah, me too."

Daniel says to everyone, "Okay, everybody in. Let's go. We have some more camping to do."

Michelle responds sarcastically, "Great..."

IN THE EARLY AFTERNOON, they arrive at White Sands. They pull up to the Visitor Center, a pueblo-style adobe building. Once inside, they watch a short film, called *A Land in Motion*, about the forming of White Sands. After the film, they visit the gift shop. Shop attendant gives Niles a Junior Ranger Activity Book, and Daniel purchases five snow saucers. Entering the park, they stop at the kiosk and pay for admission. There, they learn there are no more permits available for the campsite. Everyone except

Michelle is a little disappointed that they can't camp there overnight. Dejected, they still continue into the park.

Once inside, they begin walking down one of the elevated boardwalk trails, when Michelle says, "It's so bright here."

Daniel tells them, "You should take off your sunglasses and see how bright it really is."

DANIEL NOTICES a car passing by with "Just Married" shoe-polished on the windows and is reminded of his and Emily's wedding.

AFTER A HALF-DAY DELAY from their breakdown, they arrive much later than expected in Las Vegas. Checking in at the front desk of the Venetian Hotel, Daniel looks at his watch and says, "Damn. We only have two hours before the limo picks us up."

Emily says, "That's okay. That is enough time for me to take a shower, throw on my dress, put on some makeup, and take a shot of tequila."

Daniel responds, "Tequila?"

Emily says, "I know you don't expect me to do this completely sober. Daniel, are you certain you can handle be married to a strong woman?"

"I am pretty strong, too. I've been working out. Want to feel?" He flexes his biceps.

She says, "You know what I mean."

"Yes, Em. I wouldn't want it any other way."

Once in the room, Daniel says, "While you're getting ready, I will finish my vows."

Shocked she says, "You mean you haven't finished your vows yet?"

"No. It's not easy writing marriage vows using only Elvis song titles. Can I look at yours?"

She replies, "No, you cannot hear mine before the service. That is bad luck. We agreed on that, remember?"

"Yes, I remember. I also was not supposed to see you in your dress."

Poking her head out of the bathroom, she says, "Remember, it wasn't me you saw in the dress. It was yourself, Danielle." While laughing, she closes the door.

"Yeah, don't remind me."

Having both showered, with Emily in her dress and Daniel in his tux, they make their way downstairs. Running through the casino, they pass the bar, where Emily stops and says, "Wait, I need that shot."

Surprised, Daniel asks, "You were serious, weren't you?"

"Hell yes!"

He tells her, "We are going to be late."

"We will make it. They can't do the service without us."

Daniel joins her, and they both take a shot of tequila. Daniel looks at his watch, saying, "We have got to go. We only have five minutes." He takes her hand, racing outside to the waiting limo.

Arriving at their destination in downtown Las Vegas, they are welcomed by a man dressed in a sparkling gold suit. Opening the door of their limo, he says, "Welcome. Elvis is in the building."

Laughing, they step out and see a charming white chapel, complete with a steeple. Daniel and Emily are escorted in, where they meet with an older lady who gives them instructions. Emily looks at Daniel and says, "It is not too late. Are you sure you don't want to wear my dress again?"

Daniel, with a long stare, replies, "Don't start."

They are directed to the back of the chapel, where they take their places. Suddenly, a man with sideburns and wearing iconic Elvis sunglasses, dressed in a light-blue sequined jumpsuit with a TCB lightning-bolt necklace resting on his exposed hairy chest, steps out and stands at the altar. He could easily pass as the Elvis everyone remembers from the early 70s. The music of Richard Strauss, *Also Sprach Zarathustra*, better known as the theme from *2001: Space Odyssey* and the opening of many Elvis concerts, begins to play as Daniel and Emily walk down the aisle.

The ordained Elvis begins speaking with a perfect Elvis voice. "Daniel Adam White and Emily Rene Montgomery, you have come to the King to seek each other's hand in holy matrimony." The man in the sparkling golden suit walks over and places a scarf around Elvis's neck. "The King understands the two of you have written your own vows. Daniel Adam White, you may begin."

Daniel, looking into Emily's eyes, says, "When a fool such as I met you, I knew I could not help falling in love with you. The first time ever I saw your face, I saw the wonder of you. You had me all shook up. You gave me fever, but that's all right, that's all right with me. I knew I could never stop loving you. Emily, let me be the one. I will be your soft-hearted man, and you will be my good luck charm. With me, you will never walk alone. I will never cause you to be moody or blue. Whenever you walk by me, I will always be rubbernecking. Let's play house, but I will never make us live in the ghetto. You will always be on my mind. You will not be lonesome tonight. I want you. I need you. I love you. Please be mine tonight. They say only fools like me fall in love. Emily, I am glad I'm your fool."

Emily tears up as she and Daniel laugh. The ordained Elvis says, "Now, Emily Rene Montgomery, you may now speak your vows to Daniel."

Emily, trying not to laugh, begins. "When the snow is on the roses, I still will never lose that loving feeling. The only crying here in the chapel today will be happy tears. I won't be cruel, and I will never make your blue eyes cry in the rain. I will try not to be your hard-headed woman. We will never go our separate ways, as long as there is no monkey business. I will not walk out because of a suspicious mind but will if you have a cheating heart. I don't want no other lover, and, if I lost you, I would be so lonesome I would cry. When we cannot agree, we will always do it my way. Then there will be peace in the valley. I will be yours tonight, with a little less conversation and much more action. Always love me tenderly, and kiss me, my darling, as my blue moon turns to gold. Now, my annoying Daniel, if you take my hand you can take my whole life, too. So, take me now or never."

The ordained Elvis smiles, saying, "The King approves. Now, Daniel, do you agree to take Emily Rene Montgomery to be your loving wife in good times and in bad, in sickness and in health, for richer or poorer, for now until forever?"

Daniel says, "I do."

"Now Emily, do you agree to accept Daniel Adam White to be your loving husband in good times and in bad, in sickness and in health, for richer or poorer, for now until forever?"

Emily says, "I do."

"With the power vested in The King by Viva Las Vegas and the rocking state of Nevada, The King pronounces you husband and wife. You may now kiss the bride."

Daniel and Emily kiss, and the song Elvis would walk off the stage to, *See See Rider*, begins playing. As they reach the door, the music ends, and the ordained Elvis kneels, rapidly pulling his left arm to his chest while repeatedly punching the sky with his right. Finally, with his fist in the air, he says, "The bride and groom have left the building."

DANIEL IS BROUGHT BACK to reality by Michelle saying, "Dad, look at Nichole."

Nichole has climbed off the walkway down to the sand

and calls out, "It's like walking in snow. But, it's not like snow for making snowballs." She tries throwing a sand ball.

Daniel says, "Nichole, get back up here! You are not supposed to leave the walkway. There might be snakes down there." Nichole quickly scampers back up onto the walkway. "Nichole, I don't want to see you do anything like that again."

Nichole says, "Okay, Dad. The next time I do something like that I will tell you to close your eyes first."

FARTHER DOWN, they find a great place for sledding, and they sled down the slip face of a dune for a little over an hour.

While watching Michelle and Niles slide down the dune, Nichole asks, "Hey, Dad?"

"Hey, Daughter?"

She asks, "Did you and Mom ever come here?"

Daniel replies, "Yes, a long time ago, before you were ever in the world... We sledded here for hours, and then we set up an umbrella and chairs just like we were at the beach."

Nichole asks, "Did you camp here?"

"Yes, we did, right up the road from here. We were on a mission. Our mission was to travel across the country, seeing everything we could along the way."

Nichole says, "Just like we're doing now."

"Yep, in fact, all the places we will see along the way are places your mom and I stopped."

She says, "That's cool, Dad."

"Yes, it is... Yes, it is. I will tell you something else. While we were sledding, your mom laid her sunglasses down and we never found them. They are lost, somewhere buried in all this sand."

She asks, "Can we look for them?"

He says, "No, Sweetheart. They are lost to the sands of time." Nichole laughs.

After sledding, and before heading out of the park, Daniel asks a family who is standing next to their vehicle, "Would you guys mind taking a picture of us in front of our bus?"

The husband responds, "Sure. By the way, nice bus."

Daniel, handing him his phone, proudly responds, "Thanks." Daniel leans over, asking Niles, "Hey buddy, do want to take off your headphones for the picture?" Niles responds no by shaking his head. Then Daniel says to Michelle, "Hey, get your face out of your phone, and smile. Okay, everybody look straight ahead and say cheese." The picture turned out great, with Michelle still glancing at her phone, Niles wearing his headphones, and Nichole holding her jar with a huge smile.

Following the photo, a military jet flies over from the nearby base. Daniel looks at Nathan and can see the pride in his expression, as well as how much he is missing his dad.

Nichole cries out in response to the flyover, "That was so loud it made my ears blink!"

Michelle tells her, "Silly, your ears don't blink."

Nichole replies, "Yes they can when it is that loud. Right, Dad?"

Laughing at Nichole, Daniel says, "I guess they can. All right, everyone in the bus."

Michelle, lowering her head as she climbs in, says, "I think I would rather walk. I miss the Armada."

. . .

Outside the park, they stop back by the gift shop and visitor center. In the gift shop, Michelle is engrossed with the moving sand art, flipping it in amazement as she watches the flowing sand create new landscapes. Daniel walks over to her and says, "Your mom loved those things."

Michelle says, "I guess she had good taste."

Daniel replies, "Of course she did. She married me." Michelle responds with her usual eye roll.

Before leaving, Niles is sworn in as an official White Sands Junior Dunes Ranger, even though they let him slide on the repeating the oath part.

Not being able to camp at White Sands, they continue on to El Paso and spend the night there. Entering the city, the kids are amazed at the lights of Juárez, Mexico that light up the night sky.

The next morning, before continuing their journey, they visit the local missions in El Paso. The Mission Trail consists of three missions, the Ysleta Mission, the Socorro Mission, and the San Elizario Presidio Chapel. The missions date back over three hundred years. At the Socorro Mission, they exit the bus, and Nathan does not want to go in.

Daniel says, "Hey, come on."

Nathan replies, "Nah. I don't really feel like walking around in some old churches. I'll just hang around the bus."

Daniel says, "Okay, see you in a few minutes. You sure?"

"Yeah, I'm sure."

Daniel tells him, "If you get too hot, come in and find us."

"All right. Thanks. I'll be okay."

As Daniel and the children are getting a tour of the Mission, Nathan is leaning against their bus when a chartered tour bus pulls in. Stepping out are approximately thirty Chinese tourists. Nathan begins laughing to himself, and he goes over to the tour bus, introducing himself as the tour guide. Their English is limited, but Nathan is able to convey that it will cost five dollars per person for the tour. Nathan collects over one hundred and fifty dollars from the group.

He begins at the entrance, stalling just long enough so as not to be seen by Daniel and the kids. He begins, "Everyone, please gather around. The building we are standing in front of was the very first Taco Bell in the world." All the tourists excitedly say back and forth to each other, "Taco Bell. Taco Bell," and they begin taking photos. Nathan walks over and slaps the outside of the mission, "These walls are made of mud - mud that was brought over from China. Thank you all for the mud." He bows toward them, and they return the gesture. "The taco... The burrito..." he exclaimed. And the ever-so-delicious chimichanga... They were all invented right here where we are standing. Now, please follow me... Everyone, please keep your arms and legs inside at all times, and no flash photography."

Approximately thirty minutes later, Daniel and the kids make it back out to the bus, with no sign of Nathan. They go inside, where they come across one of the volunteers who helps to run the mission. She asks, "Are you all looking for a teenage boy?"

Daniel replies, "Yes, we are. Have you seen him?"

"Yes, he is in the church office. Follow me, and I will take you there."

Nichole says, shaking her head, "What has that boy done now?"

Daniel is beginning to get nervous about what kind of trouble Nathan might have gotten into. Once in the church office, they see Nathan with his head down. A lady in the room with him asks Daniel, "Is this one yours?"

Daniel answers, "Yep, he is mine." He looks at Nathan in disappointment.

"He was caught giving a group of Chinese tourists a tour of the mission. He not only charged them five dollars a person to enter, but he also charged them five more dollars for a picture with the standee of Pope Francis. He not only told them this was the site of the first Taco Bell, but he also told them that the body replica of Jesus in the glass case in the chapel was actually the mummified body of Christ, dug up recently by Indiana Jones."

Daniel, as much as he wants to be angry at Nathan for his actions, cannot help but admire his creativity while trying not to laugh. Even he thought the glass casket holding a wax figure of Jesus with real hair was a little creepy. Daniel also found it a little strange for them to have a standee of the Pope.

He says, "Nathan, give me the money." Nathan gives him a hundred dollars. "All of it." Nathan then hands Daniel the rest, an additional ninety-five dollars. Daniel turns to the volunteers and tells them, "We would like to donate this to the mission."

Not expecting this, the ladies look at each other and

graciously take the money, thanking him. Daniel says, "Ladies, I am very sorry for what he did, but maybe some good can come out of it with that money."

On the way to the bus, Nathan looks at Daniel and says, "Wait, so you are not upset with me?"

Daniel tells him, "I would not go that far." He puts his arm around Nathan. "Just think of all the good karma you will get for giving them the money. Okay, all aboard! Next stop: San Antonio."

BACK ON THE 10, they leave El Paso that afternoon, heading for San Antonio. Daniel turns up the radio as the song *The Road to Nowhere* by the Talking Heads begins to play - a family favorite. The girls cheer, and all but Niles and Nathan begin singing the first verse. After the opening verse, everyone points to Nichole, who lets out a deep, drawn-out baritone, "Yeah." Later in the song, for the aggressive "Hah! Hah!" sounds Niles demonstrates karate moves with his arms. Soon, the girls flap their arms like chickens to the squawking-bird sounds. Daniel, looking in the rearview mirror, smiles at seeing the children singing and laughing together.

Unable to make it all the way to San Antonio in one evening, Daniel decides to stop at another hole-in-the-wall motel. On their way to their rooms, they see a sign that reads, "Pool closes at ten. No lifeguard on duty." Then, rounding the corner, they see the pool, which is right outside their rooms. It has been filled in with dirt for what appears to be a future flower garden by the evidence of potted plants scattered around.

ONCE IN HIS ROOM, Daniel realizes the gang needs some cheering up. Since he will need to take a shower anyway, he puts on his bathing suit and tells them, "Whoever wants a good laugh, put on your swimming suit and come with me." Nichole and Niles put on their suits and follow Daniel as he walks out to the pool. There, he sits and begins rubbing dirt all over his face, chest, arms, and legs. Nichole and Niles, even with his headphones on, follow Daniel's lead, covering themselves, as well.

Michelle just stares at them from her open door saying aloud, "The poor man has finally lost his mind."

After they are all covered in dirt, Daniel says, "Follow me." They walk into the motel office, where the desk clerk has a petrified look on the face.

The desk clerk says, while stammering in fear, "Can I help you, sir?"

Daniel says, "Yes. Yes, you may. We took a quick swim and then realized there were no towels at the pool." Daniel tilts his head to one side, striking it as if to get water out of his ear and causing a large piece of dirt to fall off his head onto the floor. The clerk continues to stand there in fear. "Well, man, do you have any towels or not?"

Then the clerk says. "Ah... ah.... yes."

Daniel, snapping his fingers, "Well, chop chop. Get to it, man."

The desk clerk races to the closet, retrieving three towels and handing them to Daniel. "Here you go, sir."

Daniel says, with an enormous smile, "Thank you. Have a nice evening." As they turn to leave, Nichole is laughing, and even Niles is not able to hold back a smile. On the way out, a couple checking in holds the door for them. Daniel, still covered in dirt, looks at the couple and sees the same look of fear on their face as the night clerk had. He tells them, "Make sure you ask for towels before getting in the pool."

. . .

The next morning, coming out of the bathroom, Michelle is greeted by Nichole yelling at her, saying, "That is Mom's shirt! You take it off! You take it off now!"

Michelle replies, "Calm down. I can wear it if I want!"

Nichole says, as she begins pulling on the shirt, "No, you can't! Take it off!"

Daniel runs in, "Hey! Break it up, you two! What the hell is going on?" They both try to speak at the same time. "Wait, wait. One of you at a time. Michelle, you first."

Michelle says, "I just came out of the bathroom, and she started yelling at me about me wearing Mom's shirt."

Nichole says, "Dad, that is Mom's shirt. Make her take it off!" She looks back at Michelle, "Take it off!"

Daniel kneels down in front of Nichole, and says, "Shhh.... Hey, listen. Calm down. When you get older and can fit them, you can wear some of Mom's clothes, too. Don't be mad at your sister for wearing it. Just remember: Every time you see her wearing something of your Mom's... Let it be a reminder of how happy she would be seeing you both wear her things. Okay?"

Nichole says, "Okay."

"All right, you two hug and make up. Let's get going. The Alamo is waiting for us."

Just before noon, they arrive in San Antonio, where they check into their hotel before traveling to the Alamo Mission.

After touring the Alamo, they regroup out front. Not finding Nathan, Daniel is concerned he might be giving more five-dollar tours. Then, he catches sight of him standing with some more young people around his age dressed in black with lots of piercings. Daniel is open minded, but, even with his openness, common sense tells him this is probably not the right crowd for someone with Nathan's history to be hanging around. He calls out for Nathan, and, on the third time, Nathan responds by walking back to the bus.

Once they are all together, Daniel asks a couple passing by to take a photo of them in front of the bus.

FOLLOWING DINNER, they take a nice stroll along the River Walk. The River Walk is a park with walkways that run along the bank of the San Antonio River. The River Walk is lined with hotels, restaurants, and shops resting one story below downtown San Antonio.

Holding her dad's hand, Nichole asks, "Dad, did you and Mom come here, too?"

Daniel answers, "We sure did."

Michelle says, "This is one of the prettiest places I think I have ever seen."

Niles begins tugging on Daniel's jeans, pointing up the river. Michelle sees it, too, saying, "Hey, Dad, look. There is a boat full of people."

Daniel replies, "Yeah, there is. We are going to ride in it if you guys want to."

Nichole and Michelle call out, "Yes!" while Niles and Nathan nod their heads.

Daniel says, "Okay, we will. Hey, see that bridge up there." Daniel points ahead to a bridge that the tour boat is passing under. "I stopped with your mom right there on that bridge, under the stars, and kissed your mother." Daniel can feel a tear forming as he recalls that night.

. . .

After a boat ride on the river, they return to the hotel, where everyone settles in for the evening. Once Daniel is asleep, Nathan climbs out of bed and gets dressed. He is sneaking through the girls' room, when he hears Michelle say, "Are you sneaking out?"

Nathan says, "Shh... Keep your voice down. I am just going out for a little while."

Michelle says, "Take me with you."

"No! No. Shh... Are you crazy? Your dad would kill me."

She tells him, "Take me with you, or I will tell dad about your bag of pot."

Nathan thinks for a moment, frustrated, and then says, "Get your stuff."

Once outside, Nathan makes a phone call to Aaron, one of the kids he met earlier outside the Alamo. A few minutes later, Aaron pulls up with Jacob, Rex, and Elizabeth, the rest of the group from earlier.

They arrive at a party at Aaron's house. Getting out of the car, Aaron puts his arm around Michelle, telling her, "Let me give you a tour of my house."

Jacob calls out, "You mean your parents' house."

Aaron says, "Shut up, you dweeb." Michelle enters the house with Aaron, and Nathan goes off with the others.

After a few minutes of drinking a beer with Jacob, Nathan begins worrying about Michelle. He cannot see her anywhere downstairs. He asks Jacob, "Have you seen my cousin?"

"No, man. Don't worry about it. She is probably having a good time getting stoned. Just have fun, man, and relax."

Nathan goes over to Rex, who is smoking pot in the kitchen. Rex asks him, "Hey, dude, you want a hit?"

Tempted, Nathan answers, "No. Hey, have you seen my cousin?"

Rex laughing says, "No, man. I am so high; I cannot see shit."

Nathan is getting more and more concerned. He then spots Elizabeth. She asks him, "Hey, cutie, you want to go upstairs?"

"No... Have you seen Michelle?"

She replies, "Michelle?"

"My cousin!" he yells as the music gets louder.

Elizabeth says, "Oh yeah. Yeah... Aaron took her upstairs a while ago."

Nathan responds, "Upstairs?" He takes off running up the stairs, opening every door he comes across, continually calling out "Michelle!"

Behind each door, he discovers a couple making out. He begins panicking as he opens another door. Inside, he sees Michelle in her bra and jean shorts, with her shirt pulled off, trapped under Aaron on the bed, where she is fighting him to get free.

Aaron yells out, "What the hell, dude! Get out of here! This is my room! Get your own!"

Nathan runs over. Throwing Aaron off of her, Nathan tells Michelle, "Get your shirt on!"

Aaron says, "Dude, what the hell!"

Nathan tells him, "She is only thirteen!"

Aaron replies, "So, she is old enough!"

Nathan punches Aaron, knocking him to the ground. Then he takes Michelle by the hand, running down the stairs. Aaron follows them, yelling at the people downstairs, "Get them out of my house!"

The music stops as everyone stands around watching to make sure they leave. On the way out, Nathan reaches in his pocket, removing the bag of marijuana and looking at it before throwing it on the ground.

ONCE DOWN THE STREET, Nathan calls a cab that takes them back to their hotel. Daniel is waiting up for them outside their room. Michelle runs up to him and hugs him. Then, when Nathan walks up, Daniel pushes him up against the wall and gets right up in his face.

Nathan says, "I'm sorry. I'm sorry..."

Michelle speaks up, "Dad, it's not his fault. I made him take me. I told him if he didn't, I would wake you up and tell you he was sneaking out."

Daniel, keeping a tight grip on Nathan's shoulders against the wall, tells him, "If you want to screw up your life, just keep going down this path you are on. But if you ever, ever, involve any of my kids in any of your misadventures again, it will be the last thing you ever do. Do you understand me? I said, do you understand me?"

Nathan replies, "Yes, sir, I understand."

"If you want to do this kind of crap, I can put you on the first plane home tomorrow morning so you can go back to screwing up your life. Is that what you want?"

After a long pause, Nathan answers, "No... No."

Daniel says, "Both of you, get in your beds and go to sleep."

The two of them walk away, returning to their rooms. On the way, Nathan stops Michelle and says, "Thank you for defending me with your dad and not mentioning the pot."

Michelle replies, "You deserve much more than that.

Thank you for rescuing me. I should not have made you take me. That was my fault."

Nathan says, "No, all the fault is mine. I shouldn't have gone to begin with. I put you in danger, and I am truly sorry." Nathan hugs her.

THE NEXT MORNING, they hit the road, reaching New Orleans late in the afternoon. On the way to their hotel, while stuck in traffic, Daniel sees an exit sign for a hospital. His thoughts drift back to the days of Emily's treatments.

AFTER THE FIRST few weeks of chemo, radiation, and medication, Emily finds herself at the hospital to have a port placed in her chest. This way, they can administer the chemo through a needle into the port without continuing to poke her veins constantly. Following the port incision, Emily waits in her hospital room. Although this is normally an outpatient procedure, Dr. Patel wants to keep her overnight to run some tests. Daniel walks in, carrying a huge, stuffed toy dolphin.

Laughing, Emily says, "Oh my god. That is the largest one you have ever gotten me."

"I thought you would like it."

Emily says, "Remember when you used to bring me one every time that I was sick?"

"Yep. I also remember flu season one year, when I told you that if you keep this up, you could open your own Toys R Us."

She replies, "Yeah, and you told me you thought I was getting sick on purpose."

"How are you feeling, Em?"

"I am just depressed, Daniel. I feel like I have become such a burden on all of you."

"Em, you will never be a burden on us. We are all in this together. Cancer is a family disease, and together we will beat it. Remember, giving up is not an option."

She says, "Fuck cancer! I feel like there is a bomb in my body that could go off at any time. It is like an uninvited guest that will not fucking leave."

"I got something I think will cheer you up."

"Oh yeah?"

Daniel walks over to the door and waves down the hall. In walks Michelle, Nichole, and Niles. They all scream out, "Mommy!" and they all run up to her. All of them start talking at once.

Emily says, "Hold up. Michelle, you first."

Michelle says, "Mom, I love you. How do you feel?"

Emily responds, "Okay."

Nichole speaks up, handing her a piece of paper, "Here, I drew this for you."

Emily looks at the drawing Nichole made of the family at the beach. "It is beautiful."

Niles says, "Here, Mommy, I colored this for you."

Emily, even though she could not make out exactly what it is, smiles and says, "Oh, that is so pretty." Niles and Nichole crawl up into bed with her - Niles on her right and Nichole to her left.

Nichole hands her a Peter Pan book and asks, "Mommy, will you read to us?"

"Yes, I will." Emily opens the book, and she looks over at Daniel, smiling and trying not to cry. She mouths, "I love you. Thank you."

The next morning, Dr. Patel enters the room. "Hello, Emily. I hope you are comfortable."

Emily replies, "I suppose I am as comfortable as I can be for being in a hospital room."

"I have gone over your recent tests, and so far the chemo is not responding." Emily lets out a sigh of frustration and anger. "We are switching to a different chemo regimen of TC/TCH. We are going to get more aggressive, increasing your cycles."

Emily asks, "When are we going to start?"

"Immediately, Emily."

"So, I guess we regroup and go back into battle."

Dr. Patel replies, "Yes."

After leaving the hospital, Emily says, "Daniel, I want to go get my head shaved."

Daniel responds, "Are you serious?"

"Yes. I do not want clumps of hair to start coming out in the shower. It would give me a feeling of defeat. I want to shave my head, like a warrior going into battle. I want my hair to come out on my terms."

He says, "Let's do it together. If you do yours, I will do mine."

"Really?" Emily covers her mouth and tries not to cry.

"Hell yeah."

Daniel felt that if he also shaved his, it would help to make her like she is not in this alone. What the head shaving could not help, however, was her loss of appetite, the nausea, the vomiting, and the fatigue. The weeks passed, and, as the treatments increase, Daniel can see how they are wearing Emily down.

After eighteen weeks of aggressive treatments, as well as much tweaking to her medication, they wait patiently in Dr. Patel's exam room.

Emily says, "I so miss the taste of key lime pie. I guess, even more, I miss wanting key lime pie." Emily has lost more than thirty pounds. Instead of missing food, she misses the desire for food. Looking at Daniel, she tells him, "Thank you for taking the phone away from me earlier."

"You are welcome."

She tells him, "Any longer, and I would have started screaming at her. My mother just does not understand. I have no desire to eat. Food does not taste or smell the same. She keeps on accusing me of refusing to eat, thinking I have given up on life. She talked about coming here next week to help you take care of me. If she starts in, I might kill her."

"Not if I do it first. She has her mind set that I am not taking very good care of you."

She tells Daniel, "Yeah, well, we both know that isn't true. Thank you, baby."

Dr. Patel enters the room and says, "Hello, Emily... Mr. White."

Emily says, "Hello, doctor. Please have good news."

Dr. Patel sits next to Emily. She places her hand on Emily's knee, looking her directly in the eyes. Emily knows by this action the doctor does not have good news. There is a long complete silence in the room. A tear rolls down Emily's cheek, as neither of them blink or lose eye contact. After what seems like an eternity, Dr. Patel speaks, and Emily's tears fall more rapidly. "Emily, we have tried seven different combinations of chemo with no change in responsiveness, and your cancer has not responded to the radiation treatments. Most doctors struggle discussing the prognosis with their patients. They like to wait for the patient to ask. As I told you in the beginning, I promised to always be up front and honest with you. Many doctors will keep trying to increase treatments long after they should."

Emily asks, "Doctor, what are you saying?"

"Emily, you have the most aggressive cancer I have seen in my seventeen years as an oncologist. Whether we continue treatments or not, it is terminal. The best I can give you is six months to live."

Emily and Daniel both break down at the same time, though Daniel tries his hardest to be strong for her. Emily says, "I don't want to die."

Dr. Patel tells her, "I am so sorry, Emily. You have fought so hard and have held up so strong."

Trying not to choke up, Daniel asks, "What now?"

Dr. Patel replies, "Like I said, many doctors continue treatment up to the end. In my experience, by stopping your treatment you can live weeks to months longer with less stress on your mind and body. This would give you a chance to bond with a hospice caregiver, something that has shown to ease a patient's remaining time. It also helps the family members emotionally. I cannot tell you what to do, but I do think your quality of life will be improved without any more treatments. Emily, it is your decision to make. Do you want to stop treatments?"

Emily, in tears, cannot speak and simply nods her head yes.

"I will have the nurse contact hospice, and someone from there will contact you." Dr. Patel is having difficulty holding back her tears, as well. "Again, Emily, I am so sorry."

Emily says, "Thank you." Daniel is holding her while she crumbles into tears again.

THEY MAKE one last trip to the hospital a few weeks later, when there is fear of Emily possibly having a blood clot. Emily is in the hospital bed, struggling to breath, so the nurse comes in and turns up Emily's oxygen.

Daniel walks over to the window and says, "It's too fucking stuffy in here! You need more air. These damn windows don't open!" In frustration he begins hitting the glass. "Why do they put them in if they aren't supposed to open?"

Emily calls out to him, "Daniel! Daniel!" Finally, she gets his attention. "Come sit next to me." Both are in tears as she holds him against her chest.

"I love you, Daniel."

"I love you, too, Em."

With tears in his eyes, Daniel hears Michelle call out, "Dad, the light is green!"

Daniel responds, "Thanks." He collects his emotions, and he proceeds through the streetlight in downtown New Orleans on their way to the hotel.

After checking into their room, they go to Arnaud's for dinner. Walking in, Nichole, pulling on Daniel's sleeve, says, "Dad?"

"Daughter?"

She says, "Now I know why you made us dress up. This place is fancy."

Michelle tells her, "Just act like you have been here before."

Daniel says, "Good advice."

Michelle says, "I learned that from Mom."

Daniel tells her, "I know. She said, 'Everywhere you go, always act like you have been there before. Walk in like you are a star. Everyone there is waiting on you to see how it is done. If you do that, you will always be confident.' She was really smart."

Nichole says, "Yes, she was. One day, I will be smart like her."

Michelle tells her, "I doubt that."

Daniel says, "Okay, you two. No arguing allowed. Nichole, I think you are well on your way."

After dinner, they take a quick stroll through the French Quarter. Pointing at a building, Daniel tells them, "See that shop over there. Your mom and I went in there, and she picked up a voodoo doll and said it looked like me. She pushed a needle through its heart. When she did, I let out a scream, collapsing on the floor, holding my chest, and playing dead." Nichole and Michelle are both laughing at him. "She jumped and screamed. For a brief moment, she thought it was real and that she had killed me." Even Nathan and Niles are smiling.

Back at the hotel, as everyone is winding down for the evening, Daniel is searching for Michelle. He calls her phone, and it rings in her room. He thought it was strange for her to go anywhere without her phone.

He asks, "Hey, Nichole, have you seen Michelle?"

Nichole says, "Yeah, Dad. She said she was going to get some ice. I wanted to go, but she said she wanted to go alone."

Daniel checks on their floor for her but does not find her anywhere. Getting a little nervous, he decides to go downstairs and see if anyone at the front desk has seen her come through. Then, he will work his way back up. While nervously pushing the button for the elevator, he hears someone crying in the stairwell. Immediately, he knows it is Michelle. Opening the door, he finds her sobbing uncontrollably. She tries to stop quickly as she hears the door open. Daniel sits down beside her on the stairs and puts his arm around her. Michelle leans into his chest.

He asks, "How are you doing, Sweetheart?"

"I am just sad."

"Do you want to talk about it?"

Michelle says, "Today is the anniversary of Mom's death."

"I know, Sweetheart."

"I am having a hard time remembering when there was no sadness. It's not fair. Why did she have to die?"

Daniel replies, "To answer that, one would have to have the answer to the whole meaning of life question. All we really know is that every living thing must die someday. I would be lying if I told you there will not be even more loses for you ahead in life."

She says, "Death is stupid. Cancer is stupid, too. I am tired of people telling me she is no longer in pain and she is in a better place. I want her here."

"I tried so hard through all of this to protect you, your sister, and your brother. I did all the reading about what to expect. I thought I was ready, but nothing could have prepared me for the actual experience of it all. I am not going to tell you I know how you feel. I don't know, but I do know how difficult it is. I lost both of my parents at a young age, and I loved your mother more than life itself. But, no one can understand how another person actually feels. We are all unique, and we all have to grieve in our own way. When my parents died, I was told that in life you truly grow up the day your parents die. I have seen you mature over the last year far faster than a little thirteen year old ever should."

She says, "I just feel like... like there is this void in my heart."

"I lost a part of myself, too, when we lost your mom."

"This void, though... I cannot seem to fill it."

Daniel tells her, "Nor should you. You love her just as much now as you did when she was here. Do not try to let anything else fill that hole. Let it just fill with your love for her."

"I want so badly to show how much I miss her, but I am afraid how much it will hurt."

He says, "I still cry at times when I think of my mom and dad. How I wish they could have known you guys. As hard as I have tried to protect you all - to try and fix this - I realized there is no fix. There are no words, no actions, nothing other than to just be here for you."

"I miss her so much, Dad. When will this stop hurting so much?"

"There is no set time, Sweetheart. It may get better next month, next year, or never. The key is to let it happen. Do not hold in anything. Do not internalize it. Let it go."

"Thank you for listening, Dad."

"You are welcome, Sweetheart. I love you so much." Daniel hugs her tight. "Let's get to bed."

Looking down at the bucket sitting next to her, she says, "Instead of ice, I now have a bucket of water."

Taking it from her, Daniel tells her, "Let me get the ice, and you go get ready for bed."

"Thank you, Dad. I love you."

"I love you, too."

After Michelle exits the stairwell, Daniel collapses against the wall in tears. "Em, if you can hear me, please know I am doing the best I can. Please help pull me through this. I miss you so much, Em."

Returning to the room, Daniel is stopped by Nathan, who has just gotten off the phone with his mother. "Did you not tell my mom about sneaking out?"

Daniel replies, "No,"

"Why not?"

"Because she does not deserve to go through more pain and worry than she already has had to endure."

Nathan lowers his head and says, "I know. Thank you, Uncle Daniel."

"You are welcome. Just think of her the next time you are tempted to do what is wrong."

Nathan tells him, "I haven't been able to tell right from wrong anymore, until now. I'm really sorry for what I did."

"As long as you learn from it, you will be fine. Let's get to bed."

During the night, Daniel has trouble sleeping. He is thinking about the conversation with Michelle and the day he and Emily told the kids about her prognosis.

In their bedroom, Daniel and Emily are sitting on the edge of their bed. Emily says, "We need to tell the children. They do not need to be left in the dark."

"Yeah, it is important to be up front and honest about everything. Where should we talk to them?"

Emily answers, "Some place they feel safe and comfortable."

"What about the park? They love going there."

"No, that is the reason we shouldn't. If we did that, they would always associate this day with it."

He says, "I know. Right here in our bedroom. It is in a safe environment, and they have no attachment to our room."

Emily says softly, looking down, "Yes, that will work."

"What are you thinking, Em?"

"I don't know if I am strong enough for this."

He says, "I know you can do it. Remember the day we got married and you asked me if I can handle being married to a strong woman? Em, you are still that strong woman. I know how much you love them, and, for that reason, you will be strong." She leans into Daniel's arms.

"That's right. I am still a badass, and don't forget it."

Daniel replies, "I never will."

THAT EVENING, Daniel gathers the children, and they walk into his and Emily's bedroom, where she is waiting. When they are all there, she tells them, "Okay, everyone on the bed. "All of them climb onto the bed, and both Daniel and Emily can see the fear already building on Michelle's face. Emily asks, "So, how do you think I am doing?" They all shrug their shoulders, even though no one could miss how frail she has become.

Michelle says, "I noticed you acting different today. Are you okay?"

"That is what I want to talk to you about. Your dad and I feel it is very important to always be honest with you. What we were hoping to happen with all those treatments is no longer a possibility."

Niles asks, "What about all those shots they gave you?"

Emily replies, "Sometimes treatments don't work."

Nichole asks, "What do you mean, Mommy?"

Michelle speaks up as she is trying to hold back tears, "She is going to die, stupid!" She tries to walk off, but Daniel puts his arm up as a barrier, and she sits back on the bed.

Nichole starts crying and says, "No, Mommy! No! I don't want you to die!" She falls into Emily's arms.

Emily calms her down and says, "What we hoped for did not happen. The cancer is still spreading. I probably will not live much longer. Soon, Mommy will die. When someone dies, you no longer see them except in your memories."

Niles asks, "Mommy, when are you coming back?"

"Baby, it is not like a trip."

Niles asks, "Can I see you on weekends? Tommy at school says he sees his dad on some weekends."

"No, Sweetie. When you die, you never come back. Mommy will keep getting worse until my body finally stops working. When that happens, Mommy will die."

Niles asks, "Will you disappear?"

"No, baby. I will not disappear. Do you know when you find a sand dollar on the beach?" He nods yes. "Well, at one time it was a living creature, but now it is just a shell. Mommy's body will be like that shell when I die."

Niles asks, "Can I keep your shell?"

"No, Sweetie. Niles, remember when your goldfish's body stopped working?"

Niles answers, "We put him in the ground in the backyard. Are we going to put you in the ground in the backyard, too?"

"No, Sweetie. You won't be burying me in the backyard." Nichole is still crying, but Michelle is struggling to hold it in, while Niles is sitting silently.

Michelle, is afraid of the answer but still asks, "How long do you have?"

"I'm not sure, Sweetheart. Maybe six months. Maybe longer." Their crying continues. "It is okay to be angry, upset, and sad."

Niles asks, "Will it hurt?"

"No baby. When we die, we no longer feel pain."

Nichole asks, "What will happen to us? Who will take us to school and sign my report cards?"

"Honey, Daddy will take care of you. Aunt Bev will help Daddy when he needs it. You will also have Aunt Sharon, Uncle Stephen, and Grandma and Poppy when they visit."

Michelle asks, "Is that all?"

Emily says, "Yes." Michelle storms off to her room, while Nichole cries and keeps her arms wrapped around Emily. Niles is still sitting on the bed, showing no emotion. They all can hear Michelle crying loudly from her room upstairs.

EMILY AND DANIEL have to repeat this conversation three more agonizing times. Each time, the two of them can see in the children's faces how badly they want to hear a different ending - that it all is not true.

As Daniel is drifting off to sleep, Nichole climbs into bed with him. Daniel asks her, looking at her locket, "You wear that to bed every night, don't you?"

She replies, "Yes. It makes me feel like Mommy is here. I also sleep with the little fairy that Atticus gave me."

Daniel asks her, "Did you have another dream about Mommy?" She shakes her head yes as Daniel wipes away a tear on her cheek. "You want to hear about the dream I always have of your mommy?" Nichole nods yes again. "I am running alongside her on the beach, in the waves. It is late evening. Everything is black and white, the water, the sky, the sand, everything. Your mom is in a beautiful flowing white gown, and I am in a white shirt and white pants with the legs rolled up. She is laughing, closing her eyes, and the wind blows through her hair. The waves are crashing in. Her arms spread wide. She looks as if she could just take off in flight. Then everything changes. The sky gets darker and darker. I begin to worry. My concern, like a weight, starts slowing me down. Your mom keeps running and smiling, as if telling me, 'It will be okay. Come on. You can do it.' I begin to stumble. She reaches out to me. Every time, the dream ends there with her reaching for me. I hope one day I can feel her reach." Daniel looks at Nichole, who is now asleep. He holds her, and he too drifts away, joining Emily in the waves.

WE WILL ALWAYS HAVE PARIS

THEY CHECK out of their hotel the following morning and begin their drive to Seaside, Florida, their last stop before Apalachicola. Getting into the bus, Daniel is wearing his Counting Crows concert shirt again. Michelle looks at him and says, "You aren't really wearing that shirt, are you?"

Daniel reaches down, pinching the shirt from his chest and smelling it. He says, "It is not dirty, and it smells fine."

Michelle tells him, "Dad, no one wears concert shirts anymore."

"But, at the Grand Canyon you said you liked it."

She says, "I don't know what you are talking about."

Daniel responds by shaking his head in confusion.

A FEW MILES down the road, Nichole screams, "Dad!" She is crying so hard that he cannot understand what she is saying.

Pulling to the shoulder, Daniel asks, "Sweetheart, what is it? I cannot understand you."

Nichole catches her breath, and says, "Dad, I left Mommy back at the hotel."

Michelle responds, "I knew you would do that sooner or later. Dad never should have trusted you with her ashes. We will be lucky if they haven't thrown them away."

Nichole, crying, screams at her, "Shut up!"

Daniel says, "Michelle, stop it. Sweetie, it will be okay. We will turn around and go back. It will be okay. I promise.

Just take a few deep breaths, and not another word from you, Michelle. You understand?"

Michelle says, "Yes." She then puts her earbuds back in and crosses her arms.

ARRIVING BACK at the hotel in New Orleans, they park and go inside. They go back up the elevator to their old room. There, they find a housekeeper cleaning, and Daniel asks her, "Excuse me, did you see a teal urn in this room?"

Nichole calls out, "It's not here, Dad!"

The housekeeper says, "Yes. I took it down to the front desk." At that moment, Daniel's phone rings.

Daniel answers, "Hello."

"Mr. White?"

"Yes, this is he."

"We are calling to let you know we found an urn in your room. We have it at our front desk."

Daniel replies, "Thank you. We will be right down for it." He looks at the housekeeper, telling her, "Thank you for doing that."

AFTER RECOVERING NICHOLE'S JAR, they head back out on their way to Seaside. Driving, Daniel notices Michelle has not looked up at all from her phone since they left New Orleans. He asks her, "Why don't you try keeping your face out of that phone for a while? We are about to have some beautiful ocean scenery."

Michelle says, "I am shopping for shoes."

"Shoes? You have two bags back there of nothing but shoes!"

"These are Toms Shoes I am looking at."

"Why don't you just wear Michelle's shoes and let Tom keep his?"

She replies, "Whatever." She rolls her eyes and puts her earbuds back in her ears.

Driving down the 10, almost to Pensacola, Daniel's thoughts drift back to Emily's last few weeks.

Emily, now bedridden, is in their bedroom in a hospital bed. Daniel, having just returned from the store, hears yelling coming from the bedroom. Daniel drops the groceries on the floor and races to check on Emily. He finds Emily in an argument with her mother, who by this time has pretty much moved in.

Emily is saying, "Mom, I have not given up!"

Her mom replies, "What else do you call it when you stop treatment?"

"It is called accepting the inevitable and being at peace with that. It is about making a choice to enjoy what little life I have left in me. Why can you not understand that? Why can you not accept and respect that."

Her mom, throwing her arms in the air, says, "I give up."

Emily responds, "Good. If you plan on berating me every day, then you should just leave."

Her mom storms out, "I will! Goodbye!" Little did she know, that would be the last time Emily's mom would see her alive.

Daniel goes over to Emily with a cool, wet washcloth, rubbing it across her forehead to calm her down and to help ease her tears. He says, "It's okay, Em."

THE DAYS and weeks that follow become the most difficult time of their lives. Emily begins to have a harder time doing simple tasks, such as going to the restroom and brushing her teeth. She is getting weaker and weaker with each day that passes.

Marie, their hospice nurse, bonds quickly with Emily and the children. Nichole and Niles hug her every time they see her. Marie explains to them her first day that she is there to focus on Emily's quality of life, not quantity. She says she affirms life, and neither hastens nor postpones death. Marie checks on Emily's pain level often and has Emily keep a pain diary.

Each family member sits with Emily in shifts. They all take turns holding her hand, sometimes talking and sometimes just sitting with her quietly. Daniel reads to her every night, which, along with music, is a pleasant distraction from the pain. The children also read to her as she used to read to them. Daniel sleeps in their bed beside Emily's hospital bed, which was delivered shortly after her last hospital stay for blood clots. The children, despite knowing they will soon lose her, are doing much better than anyone had expected. Some nights, Niles and Nichole sleep beside her. Niles spends hours beside Emily, coloring some pictures of her sick in bed and others of her getting better. The family, in the evenings, gathers around Emily and all go through photos of much happier times.

Some moments, her mind is sharp as a knife, and other times she is confused and having trouble focusing. Either Daniel or Marie helps Emily change her position in bed every hour. Emily is no longer able to eat solid foods other than ice chips from a spoon. As her circulation has dropped, everyone makes sure she has plenty of blankets.

She sips water through a straw to comfort her dry mouth and battle dehydration. Daniel hands Emily her lip balm. Suddenly, the pain hits her hard again, and she clenches the sheets with her fist. She draws her knees up close to her chest. Daniel asks, "Are you okay, Em?"

As the pain recedes, she replies, "Yes. How are we doing with the bills?"

"Fine, Em. We are doing fine?"

She asks, "Are the kids up and dressed yet?"

"I was just about to go do that and fix their cereal."

"Do not bring them in yet, not until I get past this nausea. I don't want them to see me throwing up. Make sure Nichole gets to swimming practice. Niles needs his hair cut, and please make sure Michelle calls her friends. I am so afraid she is spending so much time with me that it is taking a toll on her social life. She needs to hang out with her friends some. She needs that normalcy.

"I have it all covered, Em."

"And, Daniel, make sure you are taking care of yourself."

"I will, Em."

"God, I am so tired. No matter how much rest I get, I

keep running out of steam. I cannot even roll over without getting exhausted."

Daniel says, "Speaking of exhaustion, your mother called again this morning while you were sleeping. Do you want to talk to her when she calls back?"

"No. Not now. I'm not strong enough today for a conversation with her. I say that as if I expect tomorrow to be much better."

"No. I understand, Em. She is taxing on me, as well."

Emily says, "I was just thinking that today is Tuesday. I so miss going out for our Tuesday-night pizza dinners. I miss taking the kids to school and swimming practice and... all the nights you held me so tight I couldn't even move. I also miss all the nights you stole most of the covers." A tear falls down Emily's cheek. "God, look at all these bruises I still have from the chemo. Marie says we are going to break off from the morphine patches and just go with the IV pump only. God, it seems like the more I sleep, the more sleep I need."

Daniel tells her, "You are all over the place today."

"I know. I'm sorry. I think it is the morphine talking."

"Hey, do not forget: Tomorrow, we are going to make the videos we talked about."

She responds, "Yes, I haven't forgotten. I will do my best during them to hold back the tears. I want them to remember my voice and to have them for their children, our grandchildren." She tears up again. "Should I wear a wig?"

"No, because if you do, so will I. I kind of like our bald heads."

She says, "The last time I saw you in a wig was when we snuck you into my dorm."

"Yeah... Yeah, don't remind me."

"The veil almost counts, too. I think Billy really liked you." She attempts to laugh but ends up coughing.

He tells her, "Hey, enough. That is a memory I don't want to relive."

"Hey, has anyone other than Mom and Sharon called?"

"No, that is it."

Emily says, "I miss seeing Susan. None of my friends have checked in on me in so long. Even when they did, they always seemed so distant, as if I were a reminder of their own mortality... But I forgive them."

"Yeah, it is hard on everyone."

"Fuck, how can this be happening to me? My body is ready, but mentally... Mentally, I'm not prepared for this. I just have so many things to say to so many people."

Daniel tells her, "You still need to write the letters we talked about."

"Yes, I actually have started on them."

"Good. I am going to get the kids up."

"Okay. I'm ready if they want to see me."

LATER THAT AFTERNOON, Emily is lying in her bed watching Daniel sleep. He wakes and looks at her, saying, "Wow, sorry. How long was I out?"

"Not long."

He asks, "Do you need me to help you change positions?"

"No. Lying here like this is good. While you were sleeping, I was lying here thinking about Keats's *On Death*:

Can death be sleep
When life is but a dream
And scenes of bliss pass
As a phantom by?

The transient pleasures
As a vision seem,
And yet we think the
Greatest pains to die.

What if there is no difference between sleep and death, and our lives really are just a dream? So often, we let happiness and joy slip away and vanish without even noticing. Far too often, we let those moments of bliss fade into only a memory. Daniel, I feel like I am no longer afraid of death, for death is to sleep - a rest we must all experience."

"That is very deep, Em. I must have slept longer than I thought."

She responds, "No, I have been doing a lot of personal reflection on life - like, how I want to be remembered. I don't know... Here I am planning the rest of my life, no longer planning next year or next month but the next weeks, days, or hours. I don't want to spend the rest of my life in bed. I mean, fuck... This is really going to happen. When you are young and healthy, you don't even think about dying. It seemed so foreign before. Now, it seems so surreal. Maybe it is the fear of the unknown. Hell, I think I fear the pain more than the death."

"I think we all do, Em."

"Daniel, I have not told you, but, all day and all night, I am afraid to sleep."

"Why, Em?"

With tears rolling down her cheek, she says, "Because I am afraid I will not wake up." She wipes away her tears. "The books and Marie tell me to focus on the quality of life rather than the quantity. That is hard to do when I am so worried about the children. I feel so guilty for leaving them. I'm supposed to protect them, and here I am causing them to suffer the most pain they have ever experienced. I don't know what to do to make them hurt as little as possible. I am so angry at cancer for stealing away not only my life but my children's future, as well. I will not be there for them when they need me."

"They know you love them, Em, and they know this is not your fault."

"I feel so selfish here, grieving for the loss of my own life when there are so many of you who will suffer on my account."

"Em, no one, for even a second, holds you responsible for this."

"I know. I am just so angry about life ending, but I am no longer afraid to die. I know sooner or later it happens to us all, so I shouldn't be so scared of it. I just have this hopeless feeling of loneliness in my heart, even when I'm not alone. I feel like I had some kind of purpose in this world. I keep thinking of all the things in life I never got to do, like I never got a kiss from you in Paris under the tower." She begins to cry again. "Then there are all the things I will miss. I will miss the children's faces on Christmas morning. I will miss pushing them in the swings at the park. I will miss putting bandages on their little knees. I will miss stargazing with you at night. I will miss making love with you and your kisses on the back of my neck."

"I love you so much, Em."

"I love you, too, Daniel. So many moments have come to me that I have not thought about in years. Remember that time you came home early, and you heard the shower running and wanted to surprise me? You stripped off all your clothes and pulled the shower curtain open, saying, 'Here comes big daddy!' just to discover my brother made a surprise visit and was taking a shower while I ran to the store." They both begin laughing.

"Yeah, how could I forget?"

Emily says, "He said you put one arm across your chest and covered your junk with the other." She is laughing so hard now she can hardly breath. "Why did you cover your chest? You are a guy. You don't have boobs like women."

"I was just copying his reaction."

She replies, "Yeah, but he is a gay man. I expect it from him but not you."

"I don't know. That is just how I reacted."

"That reminds me of that time we were staying in that little hole-in-the-wall motel in Arizona."

Daniel says, "Yeah, I went out for ice and forgot the key and the room number."

"I heard you knocking a few doors down. I peeked out, and heard you say 'Sweetie, it's me' or something like that."

"That was it. Why didn't you say anything?"

Emily tells him, "I wanted to see what happened."

"What happened was you almost got me killed. The guy that opened the door was some kind of white supremacist, wearing no shirt, who had a giant swastika tattooed on his chest."

"I remember seeing a look of fear on your face. What made it so funny was you had just gotten out of the shower and had decided to wear my pink robe that barely covered your junk. You thought that, since the ice machine was right down the hall, it wouldn't matter. You must have something about wearing women's clothing."

He replies, "The robe was your idea, just like all the other times. I had a look of fear all right. Fear for my life. He looked me up and down and said, 'What the fuck?' and that is when I saw you and made a break for our room."

"You looked so frightened."

"Not as frightened as I was the time we agreed to keep

an eye on your coworker Patty's home and cats while she was out of town."

"She gave me a key she had just made."

"Yeah, we got there and tried the key. It went in, but it didn't work."

Emily says, "That is when you decided to check for any unlatched windows while I tried calling her."

"I found one, all right. I opened it and thought I heard a dog bark. I called out, asking you, 'Does she have a dog, too? I thought she just had cats.' You answered..."

"While I was still trying to reach her, I said, 'She didn't tell me about a dog - only three cats.'"

Daniel says, "When you were calling her, since the window was so far off the ground, I was stuck halfway in the window. I was stuck there, dangling halfway in, and halfway out. I called out to you for help."

"I heard you calling me just as I finally reached Patty. She told me the key should work, and that is when I looked up at the number on the house and I called out to you, 'Shit, we have the wrong address!' and..."

"That is about the time you probably heard me scream as a large Doberman that must have been released from another room came charging at me. I was staring him down with just my head, arms, and torso in the window. Luckily, he only got a hold of my shirt, pulling it over my head. It must have looked like I had a ski mask on. Then, I suddenly heard an old woman's voice. I couldn't see her through my shirt, but I remember her saying, 'You picked the wrong house to rob, you scum bag.' The dog almost had me pulled inside, when, out of the blue, she hit me on my head with what felt like an iron skillet. The second impact was so hard it sent me flying out the window like a home-run baseball."

Emily, laughing, says, "That's when I helped you up

and dragged you back to the bus. Your shirt was still covering your head and your arms dangling in the air."

"Luckily, she never saw my face. I still have a bump on top of my head from that."

"Oh, poor baby. I'm sorry. Maybe this will help you feel better. I never told you, but do you remember when you took me to the Giants game? You caught that Barry Bonds home-run ball and handed it to that little boy. I knew at that moment you were the man I wanted to have children with."

Daniel replies, "Really? That was a good home run. I hope you have no regrets."

"None, baby."

He says, "Remember when we used to have water gun fights every Friday after work?"

"Oh, yeah. Whoever got home first would fill them and put one at the door and then hide."

"Em, you always filled them with wine."

"Yep, and you filled them with beer."

"Then I came home one day and caught a shot of one of yours in my mouth. I was expecting wine, and instead it was water."

"And that is how you found out I was pregnant with Michelle."

"God, those were great times."

She says, "Yes, they were. Remember the first time I saw you naked?"

"Yeah... That was pretty embarrassing."

"It was the weekend after Glass Beach. You wanted to take me on a hike, on a trail you blazed, off the PCT, somewhere in the San Bernardino Mountains."

He says, "I took you to that secluded spot I found downstream from Aztec Falls."

"Yeah, we went mid-week, skipping classes because you

said it would be more secluded, and it was, especially at night."

"I remember it was really bright because there was a full moon."

Laughing, Emily says, "In more ways than one."

"Yeah... I never planned on swimming, so when you suggested that we jump in the water, I was like, 'I don't have on swimming trunks.' That's when you said..."

"I said, 'Come on, don't let that stop you.'"

He says, "That's when you started unbuckling your cutoffs."

"Yeah, and you turned around. Why did you turn your back?"

"Because I am a gentleman. Well, when I did turn around, you were in the water up to your shoulders with your t-shirt and cutoffs on the ground."

"And I said, 'Well are you coming in?' Then you took all your clothes off."

"When I dropped my boxers, you started laughing. Do you know what that does to a man's ego? Plus, it was cold, which did not help the situation." Emily is laughing now as hard as she can. "Why did you not stop me? You didn't say anything."

"Because I was in shock. I thought you were going to keep your boxers on." She is laughing so hard now that she starts crying, and Daniel joins her. "I must say, I was not disappointed."

"Yeah, thanks. You waited until I got in the water to stand completely up, letting me see your strapless bathing suit. I thought you were skinny dipping. You didn't tell me you had a bathing suit under your clothes."

"You said we were going to a location near Aztec Falls. So, of course... Why wouldn't I wear a swimming suit?"

Daniel replies, "I don't know."

"I remember when we were eating our first meal ever as a couple in our first apartment."

"Yeah, it was Thanksgiving, and you burned the turkey, and..."

She says, "And we ended up having peanut butter and jelly sandwiches with wine."

"And you said we didn't need a turkey anyway because you married one."

"That was the night, Daniel, you said, 'One day we will look back with fondness and realize that these were the best days of our lives.' Daniel, you were right."

"Yes, Em, they were. Remember that time I hired the Elvis impersonator strippergram for your birthday."

"How could I forget? I went to lunch late that day."

"Yeah, he was supposed to walk into your office during your lunch break."

Emily responds, "Instead, he walked in while I was preparing a closing on a house with a young preacher and his pregnant wife. He looked like the later 70s large Elvis, with sideburns and all. He had on a white sequined jumpsuit that came off in one swoop, leaving him standing there in only a thong hidden under his belly. All the while, he was dancing and singing, 'I am a hunk of birthday love.' I thought the wife was going to go into labor right there. It took me a half hour to calm them down." They both are laughing so hard they start crying again.

"Then, there was the proposal."

She says, "That is the best memory of all. That was your first trip to Florida and the first time to meet my family."

"Yeah, but don't forget the week before, when that morning you told me you had a dream that I proposed to you."

"Yes, you told me maybe that night I would find out what that dream meant. I thought for sure you were going to propose to me that night at dinner."

"I had the ring, but I was saving it, so I..."

"You gave me a present to open. I thought, 'Well, here it is.' I opened the box and inside was a..."

"Inside was a book on the meaning of dreams." They both laugh. "But then we made our trip to Florida."

"Do you remember my dad when we first got there?"

Daniel says, "As soon as we walked in, you introduced me, and your dad said, 'You were wrong. He is handsome.' I remember wondering if he was serious."

"Then, at dinner that night, you thought you were sitting at the end of the table playing footsie with me."

"Yeah, I looked to my left, and your brother was smiling at me. I looked under the table, and it was his leg - and not yours - I was stroking with my foot."

"Then the next day you and my dad went to Tallahassee to a football game."

"But, my main reason was to talk to your dad about proposing to you. He gave me his approval. The next day, while you were out with your mother, I went to the dog groomer, where you were going to pick up your family's dog on the way home. I went in and said, 'I want this envelope and this ring attached to the Montgomery dog's collar.' Inside the envelope was a letter asking you to marry me.

"Yeah, and when we got home with the dog, you kept asking if there was anything I wanted to talk about. I was actually getting a little annoyed with you about it."

"Then, you got a call from your cousin, saying she was just proposed to by her boyfriend, and she said yes."

"She told me she went to get her dog from the groomer,

and there was a note and a ring attached. She said her boyfriend's nervousness seemed so cute."

"Yeah, what were the chances that two people with the same last name would have their dogs at the groomers at the same time."

"Well, her boyfriend never fessed up. They are still married, and she still doesn't know the truth."

"After that, I ran back up to Tallahassee to get another ring. By that time, we were staying in the beach house. The next evening, I placed a proposal note in a bottle and attached the ring to the neck with a ribbon. Then, I placed it on the beach in front of the house. I paid a little kid ten bucks to watch the bottle and not let anyone else pick it up. When you got out of the shower, I asked you to go with me on an evening beach stroll. We walked up to where the bottle was, and it was gone. The little boy was still there. I walked over to where he was standing. I asked him what happened to my bottle. He said, 'It washed out to sea.' So, I asked him, why did you not go after it. He told me, 'I can't swim, and, besides, you only paid me ten dollars to watch it. That would have taken twenty, easy.' I called him a little jerk, asking for my ten bucks back. Then, he started kicking sand on me, and I started kicking it on him. That is when the little shit kicked me in the shin, and he ran off."

"I remember wondering what the kid did. I was watching you get into a fight with what appeared to be a fourth grader. For a moment, I had serious reservations, and I was rethinking the whole Giants game home-run ball."

"Well, I got your dad to say he needed to go to Tallahassee again."

"Yeah, my mom started thinking he had a girlfriend up there."

"I picked out ring number three, and I snuck out early

the next morning before sunrise. I wrote, 'Will You Marry Me?' in the sand. I asked you out for a morning sunrise walk on the beach. When we got to the place where I had written it the sand, the tide had washed most of it away. You said, 'Hey, look. Somebody wrote Wi Ma Me, in the sand.'"

"Then, I said it must have been written by someone retarded."

"That was the last straw. I had no more money for rings. I stood in front of you, dropping to one knee, the good one, and said, 'Em, the only thing more beautiful than this sunrise is you. I want to spend the rest of my life gazing upon that beauty. Emily Rene Montgomery, will you marry me?' And you said..."

"I said, 'Yes Annoying Daniel, I will.'" She begins to cry, and she sees a tear falling down Daniel's cheek. "Thank you, Daniel, for an amazing life."

The following day, Daniel has an idea and begins his plans immediately. He starts by calling a friend, Steve Anderson. Steve is a local artist who specializes in metal sculptures. Daniel then meets with the children to discuss the plan, and they all go out shopping while Marie stays with Emily.

After several days of planning and shopping, they are at home waiting on Steve to deliver the last piece of the puzzle. Steve pulls up and honks his horn. With the help of three workers who he brought along, they unload two scaled-down replica sections of the Eiffel Tower's legs. They are approximately eight feet tall, and, when placed side by side, they form a six-and-a-half-foot-tall archway, ten feet across. The workers move them into the living room, where Daniel has had all the furniture removed.

Daniel had built a seven-foot-tall, eight-foot-wide square frame out of two by fours. Three feet up, Daniel has added a fifth two by four across the frame. He has attached cardboard to the front of the frame, and he and the kids had painted red bricks, a door, and two windows on it. Once the paint had dried, he attached two rectangular flower boxes below the windows. He had bought several white ceiling fan blades from the local Habitat for Humanity store and painted half green. Daniel attached the fan blades across the top of the frame, pointing downward, for an awning. Under the awning, the kids had painted "Café de Paris" on the back of Michelle's science-fair board. After adding fake flowers to the flower boxes, the café was complete.

They bring in a black iron table and two black iron chairs from their deck, placing them in front of the cafe. Nichole drapes an elegant white tablecloth over the table. Michelle wheels in Emily's bicycle, placing a red and white checkered tablecloth, baguettes, and grapes in its basket. Daniel and Nichole set up two five-foot-tall black electric streetlamps. Daniel places a large, four-foot-in-diameter, 3D, glow-in-the-dark moon on the wall behind the tower. Then, with Niles spotting him on the ladder, he paints tiny stars on the ceiling with fluorescent paint, representing the night sky. Next, Daniel takes the kids' lemonade stand and attaches to the side two large spoked cardboard wheels that the kids had made. They place striped drapes over the top of it for a roof, and the kids paint a sign that reads "Pastry Cart." Daniel hides a flashlight, strategically placed to give the tower legs the appearance of stretching into the night sky. Michelle adds a sign on an easel that reads "Bonjour" facing Emily's bedroom. The kids drape fake ivy and string white Christmas lights around the room for the final touches.

The following evening, it is time for the show to begin. Nichole sets a bottle of sparkling grape juice and wine glasses on the café table. The children wear fake mustaches - all except Niles, who, when no one was paying attention, drew one above his lip with a Sharpie. Donning black berets, Daniel asks, "Okay, is everybody ready?"

Everyone calls out, "Yes!"

Daniel goes into their bedroom and tells Emily, "Hey, Beautiful, the kids and I have something we want you to see."

Emily says, "This sounds like a surprise."

Daniel helps Emily into her wheelchair, steering her to the living room. As she sees the "Bonjour" sign, Daniel says, "You know, we never got to go to Paris, so the kids and I brought Paris to you." Seeing the tower, the café, and the beautiful night sky, Emily covers her mouth, and she begins to laugh and cry at the same time.

Michelle and Nichole say to her, "Bonjour, madam," directing her toward the café. There, Niles is trying to juggle three ping pong balls, pretending to be a street entertainer.

Emily tells everyone, "Thank you." All the kids hug her, and she notices Niles's mustache, "Oh my gosh. Is that what I think it is?"

Daniel answers, "Yeah, before I could hand out the fake mustaches, the little man drew his on with a Sharpie. The good news is that it should be gone before school."

Emily says, "Oh my gosh, the ceiling is so beautiful. You guys did an amazing job."

Nichole asks, "So, Mommy, do you feel like you are in Paris?"

Emily replies, "Yes... Yes, I do."

Daniel wheels her under the tower legs. Supporting her, he helps her stand, holding her up. He says, "You always told me that one day you wanted me to kiss you under the Eiffel Tower." He slowly kisses Emily, just as he did the first time on Glass Beach.

DANIEL IS PULLED BACK into reality by Nichole calling out, "Dad, look at the ocean!"

Michelle asks, "Are we there yet?"

Daniel responds, "I expected that question from Nichole but not you. Not much farther."

Nichole says, "I'm so excited."

Michelle looks at her and says, "Why are you happy all the time?"

Nichole responds, "Because I want to be. No one has to be sad. You can be happy instead, if you let yourself be."

BY THE SEASIDE

After a three-and-a-half-hour drive, they finally arrive in Seaside. Michelle says, "This town is so beautiful. I would like to live here someday."

Nichole says, "Not me. I am a California girl." She then starts singing the Beach Boys song.

They pull up to their Aunt Sharon and Uncle Robert's beach home. Daniel says, "Okay, everybody out."

Nichole says, "Good. I have to pee."

Michelle responds, "You always have to pee."

Nathan chimes in, "My legs have forgotten how to walk."

Sharon comes out to greet them. Hugging Nichole first, she says, "You have grown so much." Then, she hugs Michelle, saying to her, "And look at you big girl." Turning to Niles, she asks, "How is my little man? You all are growing up so fast." She asks, while hugging Nathan, "How is your mom?"

Nathan replies, "She is doing well."

Nichole says, "I love you, Aunt Sharon."

Sharon responds, "I love you, too, Little Bit." She then hugs Daniel. "How have you been doing?"

Daniel replies, "I suppose the best that can be expected."

"I know; it has been so hard on everyone. Grab all your stuff, guys, and come on in. I will show you to your rooms."

Daniel asks, “Are you sure we aren’t imposing?”

She says, “No... nonsense. There is no need to drive the rest of the way today.” Once inside, Sharon calls out, “Sara! Robbie! Your uncle and cousins are here!” Robert and Sharon’s fourteen-year-old daughter Sara and their twelve-year-old son Robbie come down the stairs. “You two, show your cousins to their rooms.” The kids follow Sara and Robbie up the stairs.

Sharon asks Daniel, “Do you want some water or a beer?”

Daniel tells Sharon, “A beer sounds great, but what I could sure use first is a shower.”

She replies, “Upstairs, it is the second door on the left.” She adds, “Don’t worry. Stephen isn’t here.” She laughs.

Daniel responds, “Ha ha. Very funny. I guess everyone has heard that story.”

A COUPLE HOURS LATER, Robert makes it home from work, and they all enjoy a nice dinner together.

Following dinner, Sharon asks Daniel, “You want to take a walk on the beach?”

Daniel responds, “Sure. Kids, I will be back in a few! I am going to take a walk with Aunt Sharon.”

Nichole runs up, asking, “Can I go!”

Sharon says, “No, Honey. I need to talk to your daddy about grown up stuff. I’m sorry.”

Nichole puts her head down in disappointment and says, “I know. It’s about Mommy.”

Daniel tells her, “Go play with your cousins. We will be right back.”

She replies, “Okay.”

Daniel and Sharon walk along the beach, admiring the distant lightning storm off to the east in the night sky.

Daniel says, laughing and looking at the tiny crabs racing across the sand, "Em once told me how afraid she was of those."

Sharon says, "Oh yes, when we were little, she would scream when they got near her feet. So, Daniel, how have you been doing?"

Daniel replies, "Honestly, I feel overwhelmed. It's been difficult dealing with losing Em, in addition to handling the grief of the children. It's been difficult trying to run a family and losing your soulmate all at the same time."

"Daniel, I think you have done an awesome job as a dad. Emily would be very proud of you."

"Thanks, but it sure does not feel like I have done an awesome job. I tried to keep everything the same. I wanted to get them back into their routines as quickly as possible. Niles and Nichole will hardly leave my side, and Michelle will barely talk to me."

She says, "Teenagers are strange creatures. One day, they are independent, and the next day they need you."

"That is the truth. As you can tell, Niles is still not talking."

"Yeah, I figured so since he hasn't taken off his headphones. Daniel, the best thing you can do is just be there for them."

"Sharon, everything just happened so quickly. One day, suddenly there are words and acronyms you have never heard before, and the next day... The next day you have a whole new vocabulary. You find yourself lost somewhere in the convoluted language of cancer. It is amazing how fast you learn to read pathology reports. I felt like I was in chemistry class again."

"I understand. Once she told me, I spent every moment I had online reading about it."

He says, "Just suddenly, I had to be mother, father, cool dad, and strict dad all at once."

"You've done a wonderful job."

"Immediately, I had to start planning the rest of our life as a family without Em."

"Losing a spouse, Daniel, has to be one of the hardest things a person can experience. So is losing a sister."

He replies, "It's a heart-wrenching experience. Describing the pain I feel, the words themselves seem unspeakable. We have been hurting for so long now. We knew grief before death." Sharon places her hand on Daniel's shoulder to let him know he is not alone. "I have this dream about her all the time. I see her. We are running on the beach, and she is reaching for me, but, as hard as I try, I cannot reach her hand."

"Daniel, I dream about her, too. I dream we are kids again."

"I miss her voice so much."

She says, "Me too."

"I am a little nervous about seeing your Mom. I suppose she is still angry with me."

"No. She finally realized there was nothing anyone could do for Emily - not even you. You are going to love how well the memorial site at the beach house on St. George Island turned out. Just like Emily asked, they planted a tall Mexican Fan Palm. Buried underneath the palm are part of her ashes you sent in a biodegradable urn. There is a large boulder beside the palm with Emily's words on a bronze plaque attached to the boulder. Facing it is a stone bench. She would be very happy with it."

"Good. I cannot wait to see it."

Sharon says, "They did an amazing job. I go there often to talk to her. It helps... some. I took the ashes you sent me to Key West and had them placed in a cement mixture poured into a structure for coral to latch onto and grow. I placed my handprint in the side before it dried, and it was sent off into the ocean."

"She so loved the ocean. I guess you opened your letter from her."

"I did. In the letter, she wrote that she forgave me..." Sharon gets choked up. "She forgave me for stealing her boyfriend Tommy Smith from her in the sixth grade."

"In mine, she told me she forgave me for leaving the toilet seat up during the first two years we were together."

"Good to see she kept her sense of humor all the way up to the end."

He says, "That, she did."

WHILE DANIEL and Sharon are walking back, Nathan is sitting on the steps of Sharon's back deck leading to the ocean. Niles comes up and sits down beside him. Nathan runs his hand through his long hair, as Niles takes off his headphones and mimics his motion. Nathan smiles at him.

Nathan says, "Hey, Little Guy. You know, no one believes me, but I did not steal that bracelet." Niles nods his head up and down. "There was a girl behind the counter who was helping some old ladies with some rings. When I noticed her looking at me and smiling, I smiled back and was so caught up in it that I forgot to take off the last bracelet I tried on. You believe me, don't you?" Niles shakes his head yes. "I still remember the first time I got into trouble. After my dad died, I started hanging around some bad kids. I was going out with them on a Friday night, and my mom was trying to stop me. She got between me and the door, and I pushed her down." Niles shakes his head left and right. "I have wanted to tell her I'm sorry for that so many times but never have. Later that night, the kids I was with were busted with drugs, and I was charged for the first time with possession. Now, just like then, all I seem to do is make my mom cry. I hate seeing her hurting, and it's even harder knowing it's my fault." Again, Niles shakes his head left to right. "I never told anyone, but the last time I saw my dad, we had a huge argument about not having my room clean. He grounded me, and I blew up at him. As punishment, he took away my new skateboard. I said some pretty mean things. The next day he left on deployment and came back home in a flag-covered casket." Again, Niles shakes his head. "I cannot change what I did or said to my dad. I just wish I could see him one more time and say I'm sorry. Since then, as much trouble as I have gotten into, my room has been spotless every day. I guess I just wish he would walk in, see it, and be proud of me. I keep it clean, but he never walks in. He would be so disappointed in me for all the trouble I have been in. What I wouldn't give to hear him say, 'Nathan, good job on your room, Son.' I know how hard it is, Little Man, losing a parent." Niles shakes his head yes. "I like you, Little Guy. You are like my little Silent Bob. Silent Niles." Niles smiles and shakes his head yes. "Do you think my dad and your mom can see us now?" Niles shakes his head yes again. "I do, too. Now, I do too."

LOVE LIVES FOREVER IN THE HEART

THE NEXT MORNING, everyone sleeps in late. Following lunch, Daniel and his family pack up and head out on Highway 30-A east to their final destination. During the short two-hour drive, Daniel recalls the final week with Emily.

EMILY CAN NO LONGER REMEMBER the last time she left her bed. She spends most of the time now semi-conscious, drowsy, and difficult-to-wake. Emily, in constant pain, has gone from liquid pain meds to a morphine IV pump due to her inability to swallow. She saves any movements for when she has the energy, which is not often. Muscle spasms and her restlessness take up most of that stored energy. Emily has blurry vision due to dehydration and has trouble closing her eyes. She and Daniel decide to allow only family to see or speak to her. She has begun withdrawing from people and desiring more peace, quiet, and personal space. Emily's days are filled with uncertainty, and her breathing becomes more and more erratic. She struggles to breathe, which fuels her anxiety and fear that each time might be her last. Fluid fills her lungs, causing noisy rattling breaths and gaps in between, some as long as twenty seconds.

Daniel is sitting on the edge of their bed facing Emily, who is propped up in her hospital bed signing her name. When she begins to groan, Daniel asks, "Are you okay, Em?"

"Yes, I just have a sharp, stabbing pain in my hips." She tells Daniel, taking a deep breath between every few words. "Okay, it passed. All right, it's now official. My advance-directive paperwork is complete. Since the doctor said I could donate my corneas, I included that. When it's time, I just want to go naturally."

In a calm, gentle voice, Daniel asks, "Did you sign it?"

"Yes. I also finished the letters I wrote to you, the kids, my brother and sister, and my mom and dad. Here they are." Handing the letters and the advance directive to Daniel, she says, "Daniel, here is another envelope." She hands it to him. "Inside are specific directions of what I want done with my ashes. This along with the letters... Please do not open them until after I die."

Tears start rolling down Daniel's cheek. "I will take care of it, Em."

THAT AFTERNOON AND EARLY EVENING, the children sit with Emily. Michelle rocks Emily in her arms, just as Emily did to Michelle when she was a baby. When Emily has the strength, she rocks Nichole and Niles in hers. Marie told the children Emily needs lots of gentle touching, hugging, and holding of hands. They are more than happy to oblige. Emily tries to read to them, but, due to her labored breathing and the increase of morphine affecting her vision, she finds it too difficult. After the children eat dinner, Emily has Daniel bring them into their bedroom. They all gather around Emily's bed.

Emily tells them, "I have something for each of you to remember me. Michelle, you are the oldest, so you go first. For you, I have the painting of the ocean at sunrise. I painted it when I was a little older than you are now. This is my most cherished painting of all my work. Whenever times were difficult, I have always turned to this painting. It reminds me that the sun will always rise on a new day and signal a fresh start. Every sunrise you see, I want you to remember this painting and know that all your trials and tribulations are only temporary."

Michelle, in tears, hugs her mom and says, "Thank you, Mommy."

"Nichole, for you, I have my heart locket. This was given to me by your father the day you were born. I have worn this every day. Inside I have kept a photo of all three of you. Now, if you look inside..."

Opening it, Nichole says, "There is a picture of you!"

"That's right. Treasure this, and whenever you miss me, open it, and I will be there."

Nichole hugs Emily, "Thank you, Mommy. I love you."

"I love you, too, precious. Now Niles..."

He says, "That's me."

"Yes, that's you. Niles, for you, I want you to have this kaleidoscope that belonged to my great-grandfather, your great-great-grandfather. It's really old and not a toy, so make sure you take really good care of it."

Niles says, "I promise, Mommy."

"Your father will hold onto it until you get older. Whenever you want to see it, just ask your dad.

Niles holds it up to his eye and says, "I see a pretty picture"

Showing him, Emily says, "Turn it here, and point it to the window, where the sunlight is."

He says, "Wow! It changes."

"That's right. It is made of brass, and inside are mirrors and tiny bits of glass. My great-grandfather was a sailor, and, later in life, he helped man the lighthouse on St. George Island. I was told he carried this with him wherever he sailed."

Niles says, "Thanks, Mommy."

"I love you all so much"

All the children reply, "We love you, too, Mommy."

Daniel can see how tired Emily is. "Okay, gang, give Mommy a big hug and tell her goodnight. Then, go get ready for bed. After you get dressed in your pajamas and brush your teeth, you can come and give her another kiss and hug. Let's go. Move it. There you go... Don't run!"

The children get ready for bed and come hug and kiss their mom before turning in for the night.

Later that night, after the children are all in bed, Daniel is sitting beside Emily, who is looking at a book on stars in the night sky. She tells Daniel, "I want to see the stars again." Daniel stands, getting her wheelchair. He hooks up her oxygen tank and attaches her morphine bag to the chair. She asks, "What are you doing?"

"Em, you're going to see stars tonight." He picks her up

in his arms and sets her in the wheelchair." Smiling, Emily lets out a laugh that no longer has the volume it once had.

Daniel wheels her out back into the night air. She says, "Oh Daniel, the sky is so beautiful."

"Can you see it well, Em?"

"Yes, what I cannot see with my eyes, I can see with my heart."

"I'm sorry, Em. There is so much light pollution here."

"No, Daniel, it's perfect. I am imagining how it looks back home on the island. I'm reliving all those moments we had together there. I remember all those nights with the shooting stars and the flashes of lightning in the distance, while we sat in the darkness in our beach chairs."

"There, we could see every star in the night sky."

"Daniel, what if when we die, we join the stars in the heavens?"

"I would like that, Em. I would look at them every night knowing you were there." He asks, "If you could pick one to join, which one would it be?"

Emily says, "I have already decided." She uses all her energy to point, "That one! That one right there. The bright one just past the end of the Big Dipper's handle. It's called Arcturus."

"Arcturus. That will be your star, Em."

She says, "Yes, that's my star."

When Daniel wheels her back inside, preparing to pick her up and place her back in her bed, she says, "No, Daniel. I want to be in our bed tonight, with you."

"Are you sure, Em?"

"Yes, I know I'm sure." She takes the breathing tube from her nose. "No more tubes to help me breath. No more. Not tonight."

Daniel asks, "Are you really sure, Em?"

She says, "Yes." With her answer, he feels Emily knows the end is near. Daniel lays her in their bed, and he lies down beside her. She says to Daniel, "When you die, it cannot be that bad of a place, because no one ever comes back." She laughs with as much energy as she has remaining, causing her to cough. Daniel laughs with her.

"It must not be, Em." Daniel kisses Emily, reaffirming their love for one another.

"Daniel?"

"Yes, Em?"

"I'm no longer thinking of all the things I regret not doing. I'm only thinking of all the beautiful moments we've shared together." She can see in Daniel's eyes the pain he feels for her, as well as the love. "Oh, Daniel, if I could only squeeze forever into a few hours. I so wanted forever with you. I wanted us to be together forever. I wanted to grow old with you. I wanted to be that old woman with the sagging boobs and for you to be hat old man with his pants pulled up almost to his chest."

Tears begin falling from Daniel's eyes, and he says, "Me too, Em... Me too."

"Daniel?"

"Yes, Em?"

"Remember my star?"

He replies, "Yes, Arcturus."

"Yes. Make sure you never forget, and know when you need me that you will always find me there."

"Until forever."

"Yes, Daniel, until forever."

DANIEL HOLDS her long into the night. Neither sleeps, not wanting to waste another moment, as they stare into each other's eyes. With three rapid breaths and one gasp, Emily's pupils eclipse her motionless green eyes, as Emily Rene White leaves this world at 3:37 a.m. on July 25, 2015, just three days short of her thirty-fifth birthday.

DANIEL, noticing a sign up ahead for Apalachicola, knows it is time for some music to distract his thoughts. Desperately needing some cheering up, he turns the dial to 100.5 FM, hears the song *American Pie* by Don McLean, and says, "Now kids, this is good music."

Nichole asks, "What is it?"

Daniel replies, "Oyster Radio, 100.5 FM."

Michelle says, "Sounds like old-people music to me."

Daniel says, "It is better than that trendy crap they play on the radio these days."

Michelle puts her earbuds back in, and Nichole says, "I love this song." She tries to sing along, with the emphasis on try.

Passing a U-Haul moving truck, Daniel is reminded of the day they moved from their last apartment into their current home. Emily was pregnant with Nichole at the time, and they had hired a moving crew that had arrived earlier than expected.

Emily calls out, "Daniel! Daniel!"

Replying from the bathroom, peeking his head out, he says, "What?"

"The movers are here early. I am going to run Michelle over to Beverly's and will be right back."

"Okay, just make sure you tell them not to take the wardrobe boxes yet."

She replies, "All right. I love you."

"I love you, too. Be safe."

Michelle says, "Goodbye, Daddy. I love you."

"Goodbye, Sweetheart. Daddy, loves you, too."

Daniel takes a shower. Stepping out, he realizes there are no towels. He says, "Great." Waiting to dry off naturally, he leaves the bathroom, peeking first to make sure no one is in the bedroom. The first thing he notices is that the wardrobe boxes are gone. "Crap!" Having no clothes, Daniel improvises by unfolding a cardboard box and stepping into it. The box only covers him from his waist to just above the knee. Daniel walks outside to get the movers to bring back in the wardrobe boxes. On the way, Ms. Parsons, an old lady who lives next door, sees him and shakes her head in disgust. While he is walking across the parking lot, Emily pulls up.

Getting out of her car, laughing, she says, "Oh, shit. I forgot to tell them about the boxes." She calls out to Daniel, still laughing, "Why are you wearing a box?"

He replies, "Because someone forgot to tell them not to take out the wardrobe boxes."

She chuckles and says, "I wonder who that was."

After all the excitement was over and the truck was finally fully loaded, Emily asks Daniel, "Have you seen Mister Whiskers?"

"No. I thought you took him over to Beverly's."

She says, "What if he is in one of the boxes? Remember, last night he kept climbing into them."

"We need to check because I don't think he will have enough air in a sealed box." Daniel and Emily have the movers unload every box off the truck. After checking each one, there is no sign of their cat.

Beginning to cry, Emily says, while Daniel holds her, "Daniel, he must have run away. If he comes home, we will not be here."

"We will ask Ms. Parsons to watch out for him. But you better be the one to ask her. I don't think she wants to see me again today."

Fortunately, Mister Whiskers is found safe and happy

inside the back of their couch that evening while unloading the truck.

Daniel hears Nichole calling his name in a familiar tone. "Dad?"

"Daughter?"

"Dad, can we..."

Daniel already knows what she is going to say and pulls into a gas station. "Gotcha."

While Daniel is parking the bus, Michelle asks, "Dad, do we need gas?"

"No, we are just stopping for Nichole. Will you go with her?"

"Sure, Dad."

HALF FULL OR HALF EMPTY

Back on the road while driving, Daniel hears one of Emily's favorite songs, *California Promises* by Jimmy Buffett, playing on the radio. He sings along, and his thoughts drift back to the day Emily died.

That morning, Daniel notifies Marie, the doctor, and the funeral director, with whom they had already made arrangements. Daniel has the daunting task of calling Emily's family. However, telling the children and allowing them to see her to say goodbye is the hardest part. Once her body is taken away, Beverly comforts the children, and Daniel sits quietly reading his letter from Emily:

Daniel,

What do you tell a person who knows your every

thought, every feeling, every emotion, and each coarse layer of every bone of every skeleton in your closet? No one ever truly knew me like you have.

If I had written this a month ago, I would have told you how angry I was and how unfair this is - how pissed off I am with cancer. But now I have come to peace with dying. Though my life is ending, I cannot help but smile when I think of what a beautiful world you have given me, Daniel.

In the beginning, I told you not to fall for me. I was scared. I never imagined myself with a home, a husband, and a family. I was always the wild child, the one people thought would be a world traveler, a gypsy. I am so thankful you fell for me. I am thankful for our children and this journey we have taken together. If I were told I could live to a hundred if I had never have known you and I could trade our life together for another sixty-five years, I would not take it.

I don't expect you to not remarry. Make sure she makes you feel like I feel for you, like forever's not long enough. Make sure she is someone who will love our children as much as she loves you.

Oh, my love. My Annoying Daniel who kept tapping on my shoulder, you never gave up on me - then or now. That crippled little fool who almost blinded me with a rock, I totally fell in love with you. I forgive you for the rock incident. I forgive you for hitting my car with a golf ball and for leaving the toilet seat up during our first two years together. I have one confession for which I hope you will forgive me: When the bus broke down on the way to Vegas, I actually did have a cell signal. I just wanted to make fun of you in my dress. I didn't think anyone would actually stop. Those moments and more, I wouldn't trade for anything.

You have been such a wonderful husband and father. I

know we are soulmates. There is no other explanation for two people born more than two thousand miles apart - so perfect for each other - ever to have met and fallen in love.

Though I am gone Daniel, my love for you lives forever in my heart.

Until forever,

Em

ONCE DANIEL HAS STOPPED CRYING and collects himself, he gathers the children so they, too, can read their letter from Emily.

Michelle asks Daniel, "Dad, will you read it to us?"

Daniel replies, "Yes." The children all gather around, and Daniel begins:

MICHELLE, Nichole, and Niles,

I know your lives are about to change. In fact, your lives have been changing since I first got sick. Having never lost a parent, I cannot even imagine what you are going through right now. It is okay to be upset, sad, and angry. It is also okay to cry. Make sure you talk about your feelings, and do not keep them bottled up inside you.

From now on, you will only find me in your memories and in your dreams. I may no longer be there with you physically, but you can always find me in your hearts.

I do not feel pain anymore, so don't worry about that.

It may not feel like it now, but your lives will go on without me. Daddy will take good care of you. Make sure you take care of him, too. I hope your father remarries one day, and I hope you will give her as much love as you have given me.

Make sure you love with all your heart, and always treat others with kindness.

I will always be there in spirit watching over you. I will be there for your birthdays, the days you get your braces, your graduations, your weddings, the births of your babies - my grandbabies. I will always be there.

Share your memories of me with your children. Show them the love that I have shown to you.

I will not end this with a goodbye because, like Peter Pan says, "Never say goodbye, because saying goodbye means going away, and going away means forgetting." And I will never forget.

I love you to the stars and back.

-Mommy

Before the memorial service, Daniel talks with the children to prepare them for what they may see or hear. He feels this is the best way to show them how we say goodbye to the ones we love.

They stop outside the funeral home before going in, and Daniel says, "Okay, guys, listen up. Niles you look very spiffy." Niles just looks at him. He has not spoken a word since the morning Emily died. "Inside, you will see a lot of adults crying. This is what we do when we lose someone we love, so it is okay if you cry, too."

Nichole asks, softly, "Dad, what if... I mean... Are you sure she is dead? I had a bad dream last night that she was... What is the word? Cre...?"

Daniel helps her. "Cremated."

"Yes, that's it. She was cremated, but she was not really dead yet."

Daniel tells her, "Sweetheart, your mother is gone.

Inside there, we will get to see her body one last time, but she is no longer inside it. Remember what she told you guys about the sand dollars?" Nichole nods yes. "She is gone. Only her body remains. This ceremony is for us to say goodbye, for she already has."

Nichole says, "No! I will not say goodbye, because goodbye means forgetting."

Daniel agrees with her. "That's right, and we will never forget her." He looks at Michelle, who he can tell is fighting to hide her emotions. He tells her, "Listen, don't think you have to be strong for any of us. You don't. Whatever you feel, let it out. Okay?"

Michelle nods her head, saying, "Okay."

Daniel goes to the Armada and grabs something for Niles. "Hey, Buddy, here is a coloring book and some crayons. If you need to, you can sit and color. Okay?" Niles nods his head yes. "Okay, guys, do you all have with you what you want to give to her?" They all shake their heads yes.

Michelle asks, "Dad, why is Grandma so mad at you?"

Daniel replies, "Sweetie, don't worry about that. She is just hurting like the rest of us. Sometimes when people are hurting, they need something or someone to be upset with. Just give her your love, and it will all be okay. All right?" She shakes her head yes. Daniel then kneels down, straightening Niles's tie. "Okay, let's go in. Stay right with me."

At the memorial service, before Emily's body is cremated, the children see their mom for the last time. Each child has a gift for her that they place with her body. Niles places a picture he colored for her. Nichole leaves her Peter Pan book. Michelle places a page torn from her journal, which she wrote the day Emily died. It reads,

Mom,

I already miss you so much. You have only been gone a few hours. You left us during the night. I am writing this hoping in some way you might be able to read it. I didn't tell you before, but there is a boy I like from school. I wish I could talk to you about him.

I wish you were still here. Now, I will not have you to talk to about boys. I will not have you to tell when I have my first kiss. I will not have your shoulder to cry on when my heart gets broken. I will not have you to be proud of me when I graduate. I will not have you to help me pick out a wedding dress. I will not have you to hold my babies. I will not have you to ask for advice on life and parenting. I will not have you, and that hurts sooo bad. I am so sad and angry and scared because I will not have you. I want to walk into your room and see you there and hug you and kiss you, but no more... no more... because I will not have you. I regret every moment that I didn't tell you I love you. Now, I cannot because I don't have you anymore. I do have your painting and know that tomorrow the sun will rise. I do have that.

I love you, and miss you so much, Mommy.

-Michelle

Daniel does not realize it, but he is crying. Nichole, seeing his reflection in the rear-view mirror, asks, "Dad, are you okay?"

Collecting himself, Daniel responds, "Yes... Yes."

Nichole pats him on his shoulder, saying, "Dad, it's going to be okay."

Daniel smiles at her in the reflection, "Yes, it will, Sweetie. Yes, it will."

Suddenly, Michelle asks, "Dad?"

"Daughter?"

She says, "It seems like a while since we've had to stop for gas."

Daniel, realizing she is right, looks at his gas gauge, which shows a half-full tank. This was the same place it was earlier when Nichole needed the restroom. He says, "Dammit!" The bus then sputters, coasting to the shoulder.

Nichole asks, "Dad, what's wrong?"

He answers, "The gas gauge is stuck again. Dammit."

Michelle silently mumbles, "I told you we should have taken the Armada."

Daniel says, "The good thing is that we have a phone signal."

Nichole responds, "Dad, we just have to wait for Atticus to come along."

Daniel says, "He might be busy. I'm going to call roadside assistance this time."

Nichole replies, "Maybe they will send him anyway."

Smiling, Daniel says, "Maybe." While waiting, Daniel drifts back to his and Emily's roadside adventure to Vegas.

After getting kicked out of Billy's pickup truck, and after Emily's laughing fit, they find themselves walking the short distance to the next town. Daniel is still wearing Emily's wedding dress and trying to walk in her heels while carrying the veil.

Daniel says, "These heels are killing me. How do you walk in these?"

Emily tells him, "Maybe you should take them off."

"Are you kidding me? Do you realize how hot the ground is?"

"Yeah, I do because you dropped me on it."

"That is because you called me Danielle."

She laughs and tells him, "Hey, keep my dress off the ground. You are dragging it."

"Sorry."

Again laughing, Emily says, "You act like you have never been in a dress before. Why don't you take it off and put your jeans back on?"

"Because all I have on is my t-shirt, your bra, and my underwear. Remember, my jeans are still several miles back in the bus."

"I guess we didn't think this through very well."

He replies, "You think?"

"Well, if you had not upset Billy, we wouldn't have had to walk the rest of the way."

"Don't start. I am not happy with you right now."

Emily puts her arm around him, laughing, and says, "I'm sorry, Danielle. I love you."

He says, "You just don't know when to stop, do you?" He then looks at himself in the dress and joins her laughter.

After some whistles and horns from passing cars, they finally make it to the little town. They notice there is only a service station and a dive-bar restaurant.

Emily says, "Not much of a town, is it?"

Walking up to the service station, Daniel tells her, "I feel like we have somehow walked back in time to the 50s."

Emily responds, "No joke. Look how old their gas pumps are."

Walking into the station, the young attendant's face is one of fear and confusion. Stammering, he says to Daniel, "Can I help you Misses... Mister... Man?"

Daniel says, "Yes, our bus broke down a few miles back, so we need some gas and a ride back to it."

The attendant, still looking at Daniel and trying to figure out why he is in a dress, says, "We have a wrecker that we can use to help you."

"Daniel says, "Great."

"But it is out right now. It should be back within a couple of hours."

Emily says, "Not so great."

"You folks are welcomed to wait."

Daniel replies, "Thanks. You don't happen to sell clothes, do you? Men's clothes?"

Spitting some tobacco in a bottle, the attendant answers. "Nope. Just that women's tank top over there." He points to a faded pink tank top in the window with glittery letters spelling out "Not My First Time."

Emily laughs and says, "Oh, you need that!"

Daniel responds, "No thanks."

Emily says, "I am so hungry and thirsty."

Daniel tells her, "Grab some chips and a soda."

She replies, "I want real food."

The attendant says, "There is a restaurant next door."

Emily says, "Let's go." She starts walking out, and Daniel follows her.

Daniel tells her, "I'm not going in there dressed like this."

"Why not?"

"Because it is a freaking biker bar. Look at all those motorcycles. For all we know, half of the Hells Angels could be in there."

Continuing to walk, she says, "Come on. I'm hungry. Just put your veil back on, keep your head down, and I will do all the talking."

They enter into the dimly lit bar where one could hear a pin drop, and they receive stares from everyone inside. Daniel says to Emily, speaking softly in frustration, "This is a really bad idea - the worst idea you have ever had. If you lived a thousand lifetimes, this would be the worst idea you could ever have in all of them combined."

She says, "Shhh..." They take a seat on the stools at the bar. "Just keep your head down and facing forward, and you will be fine."

The female barkeeper asks them, "What can I get you gals today?"

Emily replies, "I think we would like to order some food and two margaritas on the rocks, only one with salt."

The barkeeper hands them a menu. Daniel reaches for

his, and Emily slaps his hand. Pulling it back, he asks quietly, "What did you do that for?"

Emily says, "Because you have more hair on the top of your hand than a gorilla."

Emily orders their food, and the barkeeper asks Daniel, "So, you getting married, hun?"

Emily answers for him. "No, Danielle here was going to get married, but she chickened out."

The barkeeper says to Daniel, "I don't blame you, honey. I've had five husbands, and I almost killed four of them. The fifth one tried to kill me. Take my advice: Stay single as long as you can. I'll go make your drinks."

Looking around, Emily tells Daniel, "Counting her, we are the only women in here."

Daniel corrects her and says, "You mean you are - not we."

"Oh, that's right. Sorry. I forgot." Emily begins rubbing Daniel's leg with her foot. "You really need to shave your legs."

"Shut up."

They still have everyone's attention as their food is served, and Daniel asks, "How am I supposed to eat with this veil on?" He begins trying by taking his chicken strips and running his hand up under the veil.

Emily says, "Don't you dare get any sauce on my dress."

A large man, well over six feet tall and wearing a cowboy hat, walks across the room and places a coin in the jukebox. He then walks over to Daniel and Emily at the bar and says, "Either of you two ladies like to dance?"

Emily laughs, almost spitting out her drink. She can see Daniel is rigid with fear. She says, "I would, big guy, but I have a bad ankle." Daniel is shaking his head, afraid to turn around. "My friend Danielle here may want to." Emily laughs, and Daniel shakes his head no again. "Are you sure, Danielle? Sorry, big guy, maybe some other time."

As the man walks away, Daniel says, "You are going to get me killed."

"No, I'm just having a little fun. That's all."

Suddenly, the young attendant from the service station walks in, saying, "Anyone seen a man in a dress with a woman?" Both of them spit out their drinks. "There you are. The wrecker is back."

Emily says, "I think we need to go now!" They can feel the heat from the stares they are receiving. Leaving two twenties on the counter, the two of them race out of the bar.

Just then, Daniel hears a crash and a scream. He rushes around the bus to find Nichole crying and looking down at the broken urn on the ground. Through her tears, she says, "Dad, I'm so sorry!"

Michelle yells at her. "I told you! I knew you would drop it!"

"I didn't mean to."

Daniel tells everyone, "It's okay! Everyone just calm down." He kneels down in front of Nichole, hugging her. "Shhh... Let me show you something." He pulls out his luggage, opens it, and says, "See this?"

Nichole says, "There are two?"

Daniel answers her, "Yes. When we got this, I could see your attachment to it, so I bought a second one. I filled it with sand for you to carry, so don't cry. Mommy's urn is safe, okay?"

Nichole replies, "Okay." At that moment, roadside assistance pulls up, honking their horn.

After their eventful delay, they arrive at Emily's parent's house in Apalachicola just before dusk. Emily's mom Melanie runs out to see the grandchildren with her husband Patrick following closely behind her.

Melanie starts hugging all the kids, "Oh, my little darlings, you have grown so much in the last year."

Patrick walks up to Daniel, shaking his hand and then hugging him. He speaks into Daniel's ear. "Thank you, son, for taking care of my little girl. Thank you." Daniel is speechless and only nods because he knows that if he speaks he will most likely cry.

Daniel quickly reintroduces Nathan to them, "You guys remember my nephew Nathan from the memorial service?"

Patrick says, "Yes... Yes. Good to see you again, Son."

Melanie approaches Daniel and says, "Daniel, it is good to see." She hugs him.

Patrick looks at the kids and says, "I believe I owe one of you some money because she has a birthday coming up soon. Who could that be?" he says, scratching his head.

Nichole yells out, "Me! It's me!"

Patrick says, "You?"

"Yes! Me!"

"Here you go: a brand new, crisp fifty-dollar bill."

Nichole says, "Thank you! I'm rich!"

Patrick tells her, "Now don't you go and spend all of that money."

Nichole responds, "Isn't that what money is for? To spend?" Patrick just laughs at her, patting her head.

Melanie says, "Everybody, let's head inside. I almost have dinner ready. You kids want to help?"

Nichole calls out, "Yeah!"

Walking in with their bags, Daniel says, "Thanks for having us for the night, and thanks again for allowing us to stay at the beach house."

Patrick replies, "We are glad to have you. Sorry the beach house will not be ready until tomorrow evening."

Daniel replies, "No worries. We have a lot to do tomorrow. I think we are going to grab a late breakfast at the Beach Pit. Then, we are going to the Sea Oats Art Gallery, will spend a little while on the beach, and might go down to the state park. After that, we will either grab some pizza at BJ's, some fish at the Blue Parrot, or maybe even oysters at Harry A's. I can't forget the ice cream at Aunt Ebby's either. By then, the house should be ready."

"Son, you need to slow down. You need to learn how to live like an islander when you are here."

Daniel asks, "What do you mean?"

"We don't plan what we do. We just do. We just live life. You're on island time now."

"True, very true."

Patrick says, "While you all are here, we need to get together and go to the Black Marlin for dinner."

"Definitely. I have dreams about their key lime pie."

Laughing with Daniel, "I remember that. That's why I've got two of them in the fridge for dinner."

"Awesome!"

"You are going to really like the memorial, Son."

Daniel says, "I look forward to seeing it. Emily asked that we all meet at ten o'clock tomorrow night at the lighthouse. I think she picked ten so it would be nice and dark, with lots of stars out."

"She loved her stars."

"Yes, sir. That, she did."

Patrick tells him, "I expected you all in the Armada, not the bus. Did you have any trouble?"

Daniel pauses before answering because he feels Patrick will think he is crazy if he mentions Atticus. "No, not really any trouble at all. Yeah, even though Emily always made fun of my bus, she insisted we take it. I think she wanted me to drive it because of all the memories I would have of us along the way."

"Yep, that sounds like Emily, all right. Let's go have some dinner, and then we can have a beer together." Patrick puts his arm around Daniel.

"That sounds really good right now."

After dinner, Patrick walks up to Daniel. Handing him a glass, Patrick says, "Son, let's go have a beer on the patio." Daniel follows Emily's dad, who is carrying his own glass and a pitcher of beer. They sit down at the table out back on the rock-paved patio. Patrick fills their glasses.

Daniel speaks first, pointing to the rock outdoor fireplace, "I suppose with the heat in the summer around here you don't get to light that very often."

"It is much better to light a fire out here than in the house. That's for sure. Speaking of lighting a fire, Melanie was pretty fired up last year when she got home. She was really upset with you and Emily."

Daniel says, "We both tried to explain the situation to her."

"I know... I know. Both of them could be pretty stubborn at times. Melanie was looking for someone to blame for the entire mess. She was angry that our little girl had cancer and angry that Emily stopped the treatment. Rather than being angry at the cancer, she turned her anger toward you. It took me months to convince her that you were just going along with Emily's wishes. I made her sit down at our computer and read up on the difference between the last few months of people who continued treatment and the ones who stopped and just enjoyed what time they had left. I made her understand that you did an amazing job taking care of our little girl and our grandbabies."

Getting choked up, Daniel says, "Thank you."

"I know it has been very difficult for you, but you have done a damn good job, Son, keeping your boat afloat."

"Thanks. I always tell myself I wish I could have done more, but, looking back, I just cannot see what that would have been. I suppose, though, if I had one wish in the world, it would be for more time. With my job, I was gone so often, and I missed so much time with her."

Patrick says, "That is something husbands and fathers always feel. Don't let that get to you. You were doing what you were supposed to do: providing for your family. So, how have you been doing since... you know, since...?" Patrick has a difficult time saying the word death.

"We have had a lot of ups and downs. I had no idea how difficult this would be. Niles is still not speaking, Michelle is internalizing her pain, and I feel like Nichole is in denial. Throw in my own grieving, and you have one hell of a year."

"Daniel, let me ask you a question."

"Shoot."

"See that glass of beer right there. Would you say that is half full or half empty?"

Daniel replies, "I have a feeling there is no right answer to this."

"There is. Is the glass half full or half empty? The answer is that it all depends on if you are drinking it or pouring it. It is all about perception. How we perceive something is based solely on the individual. It is as unique as we are. Your wife dies, leaving you with three children to raise on your own. You can drink in what people tell you, that it is an overwhelming, insurmountable undertaking, or you can pour your love and knowledge into these bright, beautiful children, who one day will see they had a father who, no matter how hard his endeavor, gave it his all. So, tell me son, are you going to drink, or are you going to pour?"

"I am going to pour." Daniel reaches for the pitcher and fills both their half-full glasses.

BREATHE IN, BREATHE OUT, MOVE ON

When Daniel and Patrick come in from the patio, they see Emily's mom with the children on the couch, going through photo albums of Emily's childhood. Daniel has a seat and listens intently.

Melanie says to Daniel, "You haven't missed much. We are just getting started."

Nichole says, "Dad, you should see these pictures of Mommy. In this one, she looks like a bigger version of me."

Daniel replies, "Your mother showed them to me once, my first time here, but that was a long time ago."

Looking at a photo, Michelle says, "Wow! Look how tan she was."

Melanie responds, "She loved being out in the sun. I always had the hardest time getting your mother to come inside."

Michelle says, "That sounds like Nichole."

Melanie says, "When I think back, she never once got a sunburn all those years while she was growing up."

Nichole sees a photo, and she says, "In that photo, she looks like me - always smiling."

Melanie says, "Yes, you look just like your mother. In this one, she was smiling so big because it was the last day of school before summer break."

Nichole says, "I smile that big, too, when school is out."

Melanie tells her, "Your mom didn't get excited about summer break from school like you do. She loved school and wished she could go every day."

Nichole says, "Not me." She asks, "If it wasn't about school being out, what else would make her that happy?"

Melanie answers, "She got excited because summertime meant tourists."

Michelle asks, "Tourists?"

"Yes, tourists. She had many friends who would come down with their families every year. She would see most of them only for two weeks, but when one family left, more friends would come down for the next two weeks, and so on all summer long. She loved the stories they would tell her about the places they were from. Some of the families were from Arkansas, Tennessee, Georgia, Alabama, and as far away as New York."

Nichole says, "New York?"

"Yes, New York. Their stories seemed to fuel the fire she had inside to see what's out there. I suppose it made the world seem so much bigger than our little town. She cried every year when the summer was over."

Laughing, Nichole says, "I do, too."

Niles points at a photo. Melanie asks him, "You like her bike?" He shakes his head yes. "Your mom loved her bicycle. She rode it everywhere."

Michelle says, "She still has..." Then, she corrects herself, lowering her head. "We still have that bike."

Melanie puts her hand over Michelle's. "Yes, she loved that bike. She would go to the grocery store for me, hauling the groceries back in her basket. She would put her schoolbooks in there, also, and ride down to the ocean. Your mom did her homework on the beach every day."

Michelle says, "Mom loved the ocean."

Melanie says, "Oh yes, so much. At night she would have to hear the sound of the ocean to fall asleep."

Michelle asks, "Dad, so is that why you guys always have the noise maker in the bedroom set on ocean?"

Daniel says, "Yep, that was the only way your mom could sleep."

Michelle asks, "She is barefoot in all these photos. Did she ever wear shoes?"

Melanie laughs. "I could hardly ever get that girl to wear shoes. When I did, it was only flip flops. Your mom loved having her toes in the sand."

Nichole pointing at a photo, says, "Look, sandcastles!"

"Oh, yes. Your mother made some fabulous sandcastles. Every year they would get larger and larger, and more elegant."

Michelle says, "Wow, those are really good."

Melanie replies, "Yes... Yes, they were. She stopped making those when her interest turned to painting. She always had to be creating something. Our family friend Linda got her into painting, and almost overnight that became her passion for the rest of her life." Melanie begins to tear up.

Nichole puts her arm around Melanie and says, "It will be okay, Grandma. It will be okay."

Michelle says, pointing, "Look how little she was - and already swimming."

Melanie, collecting herself, says, "Yes, we would often joke that she was born swimming. She took to it right away. She was already a good swimmer before she even turned two."

Daniel says, while patting Nichole's head, "Sounds like this one. She has never lost a swimming competition."

Nichole says, "One day I will though, but that will be okay. Mommy told me sometimes you win and sometimes you learn. You have to breathe in, breathe out, and move on. She said life is the same way."

Daniel says, "Your mom was a very wise person."

Nichole asks, "What is she eating in that picture?"

Melanie says, "Those are boiled peanuts. Your mom loved boiled peanuts. We tried to get her to eat beans, but she would not touch them. We told her they tasted like boiled peanuts, but she never would believe us."

Nichole looks at Daniel and asks, "Dad?"

"Daughter?"

"I must try these boiled peanuts Grandma speaks of."

Daniel says, "We will stop and get you some on the way back home."

Nichole responds, "Good. Thank you."

Michelle says, "Look, she had a surfboard. I want one of those so badly."

Melanie says, "Yes. I believe we still have hers out in the garage somewhere."

Michelle asks, "Can I please have it, Grandma?"

Melanie says, "We will see. You will need to check with your father."

Looking at Daniel, Michelle asks, "Can I please, Dad?"

Daniel answers, "If Grandma doesn't mind. I think we can haul it on the roof of the bus."

Michelle hugs Daniel and Melanie saying, "Thank you."

Daniel says, "You will have to share it with your sister, too."

Michelle says, "I will."

Melanie tells them, "One day, your mother was so upset about summer ending that she tried to run away."

Nichole asks, "She did?"

Michelle asks, "How old was she?"

Melanie answers, "She was about your little sister's age. She slung a bag over her shoulder and around her neck. Then she paddled her surfboard way out into the ocean. Luckily, we saw her, and Poppy had to take his boat out to get her."

Patrick says, laughing, "I remember that."

Nichole says, "I bet she got in trouble."

Melanie responds, "She sure did."

Michelle asks, "Why did she leave here?"

Melanie says, "Your mom was meant for great things. She would stand on the beach, looking out to the ocean, and say there was a world out there waiting for her. So, she went for it." Looking at her watch. "Well, children it is getting late. Time for you all to get ready for bed."

Nichole unwillingly says, "Ohhh... all right."

Melanie says, "You all go get ready. I am going to talk with your father."

Patrick says, "I think I am going to get ready for bed, too. Goodnight, Daniel."

Daniel replies, "Goodnight, Patrick." Sitting there with Melanie, Daniel speaks first and says, "Melanie, I am sorry..."

Melanie cuts him off, telling him, "Daniel you have nothing to apologize for. I am the one who owes you an apology. I was just angry and in denial." Beginning to cry, she says, "I just... I just didn't want to lose my baby."

"I know, Melanie."

"And stop calling me Melanie. After all these years, you still call me Melanie. Call me Mom. You are more than just a son-in-law to me. You are a savior - not only to Emily but to those little angels, as well. What you have been through - have endured... Very few men could have stayed as strong as you have for these children."

Daniel says, “I have tried my hardest to keep us going without her.”

“She is not gone. Emily is still with us. All you have to do is look into those little faces of these babies, and you can see Emily lives on in them and will forever.”

“That, she will.”

Melanie stands, hugging Daniel, and says, “I love you, Son.”

Daniel tears up, replying, “I love you, too, Mom.”

THE BRIGHT STAR TO THE LEFT AND STRAIGHT ON TILL MORNING

THE NEXT MORNING, after a late breakfast at the Beach Pit, they head over to the Sea Oats Art Gallery. Climbing out of their bus, they see a seagull standing near the door.

"Look. A seagull" Nichole says, pointing to it, laughing, and doing her best *Finding Nemo* imitation. "Mine, mine, mine, mine, mine..."

Daniel says, "Hey, it's Steven."

Nichole asks, "You know his name?"

"Yes, Steven Seagull. We go way back." Michelle rolls her eyes. Daniel says softly, "Well, your mom always liked that joke, or at least she pretended to."

Walking in, they are greeted by Linda Moore, a long-time friend of Emily's family and the one who inspired Emily to start painting.

Linda says, "Oh my gosh! Daniel, it is so good to see you."

Daniel says, "Good to see you, too, Linda."

She says, "Oh my, the children have grown so much."

Nichole says, "Everybody keeps saying that."

Linda looks at her, "You are a little princess - like your mom."

Nichole responds, "I'm not a princess. My dad told me I'm a drama queen."

Michelle laughs at her, "That is not a compliment."

Nichole says, "Yes, it is! Right, Dad?"

Daniel says, "For you, yes. Hey, Linda, I have a present Em wanted you to have." He hands her a flat package that is approximately eighteen by thirty-four inches and wrapped in brown paper.

Linda delicately unwraps the package to find a painting of the beach. On the beach are the backs of a woman sitting in the sand next to a young teenage girl. In front of them is the ocean, where the woman is pointing. Directly in front of them is an easel. On the easel is a painting of the tide rolling in. "Oh my." Linda says, covering her mouth as a tear rolls down her cheek. "That is me and Emily. Oh, thank you, Daniel."

"You're welcome. All I did was deliver it. Em began working on it when she knew she..." Daniel pauses and chooses his words selectively with the children present. "When she knew she wouldn't be able to thank you in person."

FOLLOWING their trip to the gallery, they head to the lighthouse. Daniel reminds them, saying, "Your great-great-grandfather used to man the lighthouse, keeping ships safe." Nichole asks, "Dad can we go up there?"

Daniel replies, "We sure can." They all climb to the top. Once there, Nathan picks up Niles to help him see better.

Nichole says, "Dad, I can see forever from up here."

Michelle replies, "No, you can't."

Nichole responds, "Yes, I can."

Michelle asks her, "Okay, if you can see forever, where is our house back home?"

While pointing, Nichole says, "It is right there."

Daniel plays along and says, nudging Michelle, "You are right. I see it."

Michelle, trying not to laugh, says, "Nichole, there it is. I see it." Nichole smirks at them and begins to laugh.

. . .

After climbing down, they visit the museum. There, the kids learn more about their great-great-grandfather. Nichole becomes a bit of a tour guide by going up to each person there and telling them of her family's connection to the lighthouse. Before leaving, Daniel asks a family if they would take a photo of them beside the bus with the lighthouse in the background. After the photo, once inside the bus, Nichole asks Daniel, "Dad?"

"Daughter?"

"Why do you keep having people take our photos every time we stop?"

Daniel answers, "Remember, when we were at White Sands when I told you your mom and I took this same route our first time here together?"

"Yes."

Daniel reaches into the glove box and pulls out a stack of photos, handing them over his shoulder to Nichole while Michelle and Niles look on. Nichole says, "Dad, you and Mommy took the exact same photos in front of the bus at every place we did."

"That's right. That was another request your mom made when she asked us to take this trip. She wanted us not only to take the same route but also to take the same photos."

Michelle says, "That is so cool. Do you think we could put them all together in a frame when we get home? All of them... I mean, could we put the ones of you and Mom and the ones of all of us side by side?"

Daniel replies, "Your mom said the same thing."

Proudly, Nichole says, "Mom thought of everything."

Daniel responds, "That, she did... That, she did."

. . .

They stop by the St. George Island Trading Company for some souvenir shopping, and Daniel purchases bodyboards for everyone. He takes the children down to the beach, where they rent beach chairs and an umbrella. They all get into the water - all except Nichole.

Daniel calls out to her, "Nichole, come on into the water. It is nice and warm." Nichole shakes her head no, looking down. Daniel gets out and walks up to their umbrella and chairs, where she is standing. "Why don't you want to get in?"

"Because Billy Ellis from school told me there are big sharks in Florida."

"Don't be scared of sharks. You are safe as long as you do not swim next to someone who is fishing or swim at sunrise or dusk. Come on."

"No."

"You are good swimmer - the best I have ever seen. You win every swim meet you are in."

"I can't outswim a shark, though."

"Hey, you don't have to. You just need to swim faster than the person next to you." Nichole laughs. "Okay?"

She says, "Okay!" and she races him to the water.

While in the water, the man who rented them the umbrella and chairs walks down to the shore with his dog. Pointing toward the man's dog, Michelle says, "Hey, look."

Nichole, who had asked Daniel earlier if the man was a pirate due to his skull cap and beard, sees the dog jumping onto a skimboard the man is throwing in front of it. "Dad, look! That dog can surf!" Nichole goes over and pets the man's dog, and he lets her try to toss the board.

The man says, "Here... Toss it like this, and he will go after it."

Nichole says, "Okay, let me try." On the fourth try, she

gets it with a little help from the man, and the dog skims across the sand. "Dad! I did it! I did It!"

Daniel tells her, "Good job!"

Michelle says, "Dad, I wish we could have brought mom's old surfboard with us."

He tells her, "I promise, we will go get it tomorrow."

She replies, "Thanks, Dad."

Daniel asks, "Is everyone having fun?"

Michelle and Nichole yell out, "Yes!"

This is the happiest Daniel has seen the three of them, since before Emily got sick. Niles actually took off his headphones to get into the water. The only thing he has been wearing today is a smile - something he had misplaced long ago. Even Nathan, who has kept to himself most of the trip, is having a blast with his cousins in the water.

Following the beach, they make a trip down to the St. George Island State Park.

Looking at the dunes Nichole asks, "Dad, can we get our sleds out and slide down the dunes?"

Daniel tells her, "No, Sweetheart. These dunes are just to look at and to enjoy their beauty. Hey, you guys want to walk along the beach up here to search for shells and treasure?"

Michelle, Nichole, and Nathan all respond at the same time, saying, "Treasure?"

Daniel says, "Yes, treasure. There was a man named William 'Bowlegs' Bowles, and it is said he buried several treasure chests somewhere in this area back in 1799."

Michelle asks, "Was he a pirate?"

Daniel answers, "Kind of. He commanded a flotilla of

pirate ships that would attack Spanish ships. The ship he was on, the HMS Fox, was wrecked here."

Nichole asks, "Dad, what does a tortilla have to do with pirates?"

Michelle laughs and says, "Flotilla, not a tortilla."

Nichole replies, "That's what I said. A float... Dad knows what I meant."

Nathan speaks up, answering her question, "A flotilla is a small fleet of warships."

Daniel says, "That's right. Good job, Nathan."

After an unsuccessful treasure search, they grab some pizza from BJ's and ice cream at Aunt Ebby's. Before going to the beach house, they make a quick stop at the SGI Fresh Market to grab some groceries for their stay. Once grocery shopping is finished, they drive past the guarded kiosk into the private section of the island called The Plantation. Pulling up to the house, a wave of memories washes over Daniel. The house is as beautiful as the first time he and Emily stayed there. They all go inside, claiming their bedrooms like prospectors at a gold rush.

Nichole, after picking hers, calls out, "I'm hungry!"

Michelle tells her, "You are always hungry."

Looking at Daniel, Nichole again says, "I'm hungry."

Daniel says, "You just ate a little while ago."

"Well, I am hungry again."

Daniel replies, "Well, I just put some food in the fridge. See what you can find. I am going to go out back for a moment."

"No, I want real food."

He says, "That is real food, bought with real money at a real grocery store."

"I want drive-thru food - the kind that is made for you."

"Sorry, Charlie. You will just have to eat what we have."

"All right..." Nichole responds, defeated, while Daniel goes out back to see Emily's memorial.

Daniel says to himself, "Sharon was right. It is perfect." He sits on the bench, facing the ocean and the memorial, while reading Emily's words on her plaque.

Never before have I stopped to think about that little dash that separates our births from our deaths. There is so much that goes into that little line - so much laughter, so many tears, so much happiness, and so much sorrow. How can an entire lifetime fit on such a tiny line? The birthdays, the brand-new boxes of sixty-four crayons, the sandcastles, the first time a boy holds your hand, the first kiss, the broken hearts, that perfect sunset, the perfect sunrise, the will-you-marry-me moment, the weddings, the anniversaries, the French fries with mayonnaise, the sleeping in, the feel of fresh linens, the storms, the rainbows, the stargazing, the births, the skinned knees, the tears on the first day of school, the smiles on Christmas mornings, the warm sand between your toes, the right song at the right moment, the wrong song, the bubble baths with a great book and bottle of wine, the smell of a sea breeze, that perfect piece of art... It's the sweet dreams, the I love yous, the I miss yous, and the letting go.

Next time you see that dash, take a moment to think of all that happened during that little line. Always live life to the fullest, and cherish each and every moment so you, too, can have a lifetime that makes your little line memorable.

-Emily Rene White

July 28, 1980 - July 25, 2015

. . .

MICHELLE STEPS OUT, joining Daniel. She says, "I heard Grandma talking about Mom's memorial. It is so pretty."

Daniel says, "Yes, it is - just the way she wanted it."

Michelle takes a moment to read it. She says, "Dad, reading this I can still hear her voice. That is something I have not been able to hear in so long."

Daniel places his arm around Michelle and says, "Me too, Sweetheart. Me too."

Michelle tells him, "Dad, I have been thinking about what you were told about growing up the day your parents die. I think the day you really grow up is the day after you reach the age your parent lived to be."

"You are definitely your mother's child."

She says, "I just wanted you to know that and know that I am still a kid. I love you, Dad."

"I love you too, Angel."

NIGHTFALL ARRIVES, and the stars fill the sky. Nichole says, "I have never seen so many stars."

Emily's parents, her sister Sharon and her family, and her brother Stephen all gather with Daniel's family at the lighthouse on the island. They all walk down the walkway to the beach, standing on the shoreline. Daniel wades out into the white-capped waves with Emily for the last time. Holding her urn, Daniel speaks, "Emily Rene White, you were born thirty-six years ago tonight. You were the love of my life. You gave me three beautiful children and a love beyond anything I could have ever dreamed. Now, it is time for your next adventure to begin as you join the sea and ride the current. Em, I will love you forever." Daniel opens the urn and submerges it into the waves. "You will always be in my heart, my love - until forever."

Leaving the beach, Daniel stops beside the lighthouse and tells everyone, "On Emily's last night, she told me that when she passed, she was going to join the stars. She said the star Arcturus was the one she would choose. It is the fourth brightest star in the night sky." Pointing to the sky, he says, "If you look up and see the Big Dipper... Now, follow the handle behind the lighthouse. See that really bright star, to the left of the lighthouse?"

Nichole calls out, "I see it!"

Daniel says, "I think I know why Emily chose this star and this night for us to be here. Arcturus is thirty-six light years away. That means when we look at the star right now, we are seeing it as it appeared thirty-six years ago, the night Emily was born."

Niles removes his headphones and says, "I see her star, Daddy. I see where Mommy is." These are the first words he has spoken since Emily's death.

Everyone stunned. Melanie speaks first, calling out, "He spoke! He spoke!" They all gather around Niles, hugging him.

Nichole looks at Daniel and says, "Daddy! Daddy! My wish on the falling star from the Grand Canyon came true!" She wraps her arms around Niles, picking him up.

In tears, Daniel hugs him tight, saying, "That's right, Little Man. That's right. That is Mommy's star."

Later that night, Daniel is having trouble sleeping, when Niles walks into his bedroom. Niles says, "Daddy, can I sleep with you?"

"Yeah, come on, Little Man, and lie down. You having trouble sleeping, too?"

Niles nods his head yes. Listening to the waves outside, Niles says, "Daddy, I like hearing the ocean, too - just like Mommy."

Daniel says, "Me too, buddy."

"Dad, I know the ocean can't speak, but, if you listen to the waves, it has a lot to say."

Daniel responds, "That, it does."

"I miss Mommy tucking me in at night. She used to sing to me."

"I remember. I remember the song, as well. Do you want me to sing to you?"

Niles says, "Yes."

Daniel begins singing the song *Morning Has Broken* by Cat Stevens, and Niles drifts away. Daniel keeps singing until he finishes the song.

Sleeping, Daniel has the same dream he always has of Emily reaching out for him. Just as before, the sky darkens, and he begins to stumble. Emily reaches out, and for the first time his hand touches hers, allowing him to stand on his own. She smiles at him, like a mother overflowing with pride, releasing her grown children into the world. With her arms spread wide, she lets go of his hand and soars into the sky - now dark - drifting away to her star, Arcturus.

The next morning in the beach house, Daniel is woken by Michelle calling out to him, "Dad! Nathan's gone!"

Daniel spends the morning speaking with the Franklin County Sheriff's Department. Since Nathan is eighteen, it is too early for them to report him missing. The family spends the rest of the day searching for him. Nightfall arrives, and Nathan walks in the door of the beach house. The girls and Niles run up, hugging him. Daniel, highly upset, says, "Where the hell have you been? We have spent the entire day looking for you, worried to death."

Nathan says, in a strong confident voice, "I hitched a ride last night to Panama City."

Daniel says, "Panama City? We have a beach right here. What... Was there another party you couldn't miss? I told you the next time you pull something like this..."

"It's okay, Uncle Daniel. I'm okay. I met with an Army recruiter today. He gave me a ride back. I am enlisting."

Daniel is overcome with pride for the young man. "Just like your father. He would be very proud of you right now."

"Yeah, just like my father. Except, instead of following in his footsteps, I have my own trail to blaze."

Daniel hugs Nathan, saying, "I am so proud of you, Kid."

Nathan says, "Thank you, Uncle Daniel. I'm sorry I didn't tell you I was going. I wanted it to be my own decision without any encouragement or disapproval. I just spoke to my mom. She should be calling..." The phone rings. "That would be her. She is getting me a flight home. The recruiter in Panama City has set me up with a recruiter back home. As much as I have enjoyed this trip, and I really did, I am taking the faster way home." They both laugh.

While Michelle is talking to her aunt Beverly, Daniel says, "I kind of don't blame you."

Nathan says, as Daniel is walking over to Michelle to take the call, "And, Uncle Daniel..." Daniel stops and turns. "If I had not been on this trip with you, I don't think I would have made it. Thank you." A tear falls down Daniel's cheek, knowing it was all because of Emily.

"You're welcome, Nathan."

THE NEXT MORNING, they drive Nathan to the airport in Tallahassee. Before getting on the plane, Nathan walks up to each child, hugging them, and says, "I will miss you guys." He looks down at Niles and says, "And I will miss you the most, Silent Niles. You taught me you don't have to say a lot to say a lot."

Hugging him, Niles says, "I will miss you, too." Then, to everyone's surprise, Niles says, "Remember, your dad is watching you."

Nathan says, "That's right, Little Man. That's right." Then, Nathan hugs Daniel, saying, "Uncle Daniel, thank you so much."

Daniel says, "You are welcome. You take care."

Nathan replies, "I will. I will write you guys." Walking away, he says, "Goodbye!"

Nichole calls out, "Never say goodbye because goodbye means forgetting!"

Nathan responds, "I won't forget!"

The next day at the beach house, after lunch, there is a knock on the door. Daniel says, "Michelle, will you get that?"

Michelle replies, "Sure, Dad."

Opening the door, she sees Linda from the Sea Oats Art Gallery with her arms filled with art supplies. Linda says, "Hello. I believe we have an art lesson."

Michelle excitedly says, "We do?"

Daniel walks up and tells Michelle, "I asked if Linda would work with you like she did with your mom."

Michelle hugs Daniel, "Thank you so much, Dad."

Daniel says, "While you guys do that, we are all going to go pick up your mom's surfboard."

Linda works with Michelle for several days, and in the process Michelle discovers a hidden talent she never knew she had. On Michelle's last day of lessons, she follows Linda out to her van. Walking back in, Michelle has a large box in her arms. Daniel asks, "What is that?"

Michelle replies, "Linda gave me a ton of art supplies to get started back home."

Daniel replies, "Nice. Go put it in your room, and make sure we don't forget it. Without Nathan riding back, it will fit perfectly beside you on the seat." As Michelle takes the box to her room, Daniel tells Linda, "Thank you. She really needed this right now."

Linda replies, "That little one of yours truly has a gift. She is far more advanced than Emily was at her age. She needs a little more practice, but she is good. I mean really good."

"Thank you. That means so much and would mean so much to Emily, too."

Over the next few days, Michelle and Nichole discover riding a surfboard requires much practice and much larger waves than they expected. The family continues to enjoy the island, but, before anyone is ready, it is finally time to begin their long drive back home. After loading the bus, Daniel takes a moment to sit on the bench at Emily's memorial to have some private last words, when Nichole walks up.

Daniel says, "What's up, Buttercup?"

Nichole says, "I guess I'm just sad that we are having to leave. I love it back home in California, but there is just something about being here that tells me I need to return."

"I know what you mean. I think your mom felt the same way."

"Dad, do you think I might end up living here someday?"

Daniel answers, "I don't know. It wouldn't surprise me. You just have to listen to your heart. No one knows what the future will bring."

Nichole says, "Dad, if the future means what is going to happen, does that mean the past is what didn't happen?"

Processing her words, he replies, "No, not exactly. Yes, the future is what is going to happen, but we cannot change what happened in the past. We can only..."

Nichole finishes his sentence along with him, "Learn from it. Mommy taught me that."

Daniel asks, "Are you still worried something might happen to me?"

"No. Not anymore. For some reason, for the first time, I'm not worried about anything anymore."

"That is a good way to feel."

Hugging his neck, Nichole responds, "Yes, it is. I love you, Dad."

"I love you, too, Sweetheart. Now go tell your brother and sister to get ready to leave. I am going to sit here for a few minutes."

"Okay, Dad."

NICHOLE WALKS AWAY, and Daniel begins speaking to Emily's memorial, "Well, Em, it has been a year now. How do you think I'm doing? I have made a few mistakes along the way. Okay, maybe more than a few... But, in your father's words, I have 'kept the ship afloat.' I just wish my first mate were here.

"This life has been a journey, and this has been more than just a road trip. Knowing you, I think you knew that all along. It was a pilgrimage for us to find the peace and healing we so desperately have needed. When you asked me to bring your ashes here on your birthday, with the route you chose and you picking your star, I think you knew what we needed to heal all along. And you were right. You always were.

"Now, we are loaded up and ready to make the long drive back home. This was when you always started singing *Going Back to Cali*. I love you, but I am not going to sing. Actually, this will be the first time I will leave here without you. But, in many ways, Em, I know that you will always be with me.

"Oh, and by the way, if you happen to know a particular fairy and wish maker extraordinaire, could you ask him to watch out for us on the way home. Thanks.

I love you, Em, until forever, my love."

Niles walks up to Daniel, smiling and placing his hand on Daniel's shoulder from behind and says, "Daddy, we are going to be okay." That is something Daniel has told him many times.

Daniel replies, "Yes. Yes, we will."

DANIEL CLIMBS into the driver's seat and backs out into the street.

Nichole says, "Dad, life is so much more amazing than any storybook I have ever read."

Daniel responds, "I have to agree with you, Sweetheart. It really is." Then, out of the blue Daniel starts singing the LL Cool J song *Going back to Cali*.

Before they get a few yards down the road. Nichole calls out, "Dad?" Daniel makes a U-turn back to the beach house.

THE END

ABOUT THE AUTHOR

Michael Combs is an author and licensed massage therapist. He attended the University of Arkansas at Little Rock and is a proud member of the Kappa Sigma Fraternity. Raised in Arkansas, he began writing at sixteen and has received numerous awards for his poetry. Now he has turned his primary focus to fiction.

Whether it involves months of research or traveling to the locations he writes about, he embeds himself into his writing. Unlike many authors who require silence when writing, Combs writes to music and has a soundtrack for each book, giving his work a unique flow. When asked about his writing, Combs like to describe himself as a storyteller, having lived a remarkable life that has given him abundant writing material.

Besides *Arcturus*, Michael's writings include: *Lost Boy, Lost Boy: Brace Yourself, The Long Road Home*, and *Twice Upon a Time.*

Lost Boy: Brace Yourself continues the *Lost Boy Series* as Mike faces more challenges finding his place in the world. Just like the title says, brace yourself. for along with his friend Keith the laughter is non-stop, and neither is his love for Gabi.

The Long Road Home is a story of returning home, dealing with loss, and finding true love. A woman discovers her heart, and an outlaw biker must decide how far he will go to heal his own.

Twice Upon a Time is a love story taking place between 1890s Paris and 1990s New Orleans. It is not a once-upon-a-time story but rather a story of soul mates, about hope, life, dreams and love – a belief love can return...twice upon a time.

COMING SOON

Lost Boy: Brace Yourself

www.lostboypublishing.com

Facebook.com/lostboypublishing

twitter.com/LostBoyPublish

instagram.com/lostboypublishing

Look for the next book in the Lost Boy series.

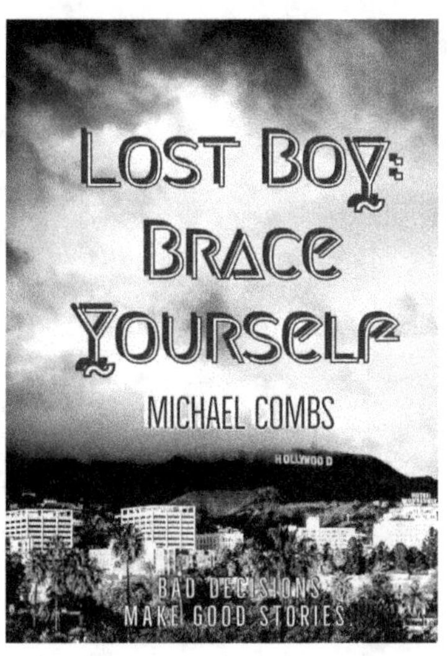

NEW BOOKS COMING SOON

by Michael Combs...

Lost Boy: Brace Yourself

THE LONG ROAD HOME

Twice Upon a Time

www.ingramcontent.com/pod-product-compliance
Lightning Source LLC
Chambersburg PA
CBHW060548310726
48982CB00008B/1051/J

* 9 7 8 1 7 3 5 9 7 0 3 0 1 *